# Seasons of Love

## Andrea Boeshaar

Published by Prism Book Group
First Edition, 2015
ISBN-13: 978-1519611369
ISBN-10: 1519611366
Published in the United States of America
Contact info: contact@prismbookgroup.com
http://www.prismbookgroup.com

# An Apple a Day

# Dedication

To my son Brian, a former U. S. Army National Guard medic, and a two-time veteran of the *War on Terror*. May you soon meet your "Talia."

# *One*

DR. BRIAN CORIDAN turned the key in his palm. It felt cold in spite of the torrid heat during this last week of June. Above him, a leafy green canopy draped gracefully over the narrow gravel driveway on which he'd parked his gray, mid-sized sport utility vehicle. Slivers of sunshine made their way through the natural arch and peppered the ground below.

His gaze slid to the rustic cabin and beyond it to the gleaming, silvery-blue lake. Breathing in the clean, fresh, northern Wisconsin air, Brian decided his buddy, Toby, had been right. This sabbatical from the clinic was exactly what he needed. Up here, in the North Woods, sitting by a calming lake, Brian could fish to his heart's content, collect his thoughts, and pray about what he should do regarding his medical career.

He grunted as the latter pervaded his mind for the umpteenth time today. His practice at the Family Practice Medical Clinic had grown old, sour, and distasteful. What began as a deep-rooted desire to help people had morphed into a dog-eat-dog business. People weren't much a part of it. Sure, he saw patients on a regular basis, but he could no longer spend much time with them.

According to the clinic's administrator, Brian was allotted seven minutes—tops—to perform an evaluation. Then it was write out a prescription and send the patient on his way.

Next!

Like a fast-food restaurant.

Medicine was all about money now, and Brian felt burned out, trying to keep up his imposed status quo. Worse, he feared the day when, in his haste, he would make an incorrect diagnosis and harm his patient. He had to get out before that happened.

But was that what God wanted?

Over the years, Brian worked hard and spent tens of thousands of dollars putting himself through medical school. The Lord guided his every step, even providing some of the funding in the way of grants and scholarships. Why would God want him to quit now? It made no sense.

And that's why Brian came here, to rest and to pray over his future. It seemed he'd found paradise in which to do his soul-searching, too. Simply imagining the entire summer here in beautiful Blossom Lake, Wisconsin, eased the stress he carried between his scapulae.

Gathering his belongings, Brian headed for the cabin and let himself in. He allowed his eyes to adjust to the darkness. The log structure's main room came into focus. It was divided into a living room and kitchen area. Off to the side were two small bedrooms. Since one sported bunk beds, Brian opted for the other room and its full-size bed.

He let the heavy duffle bag drop from his shoulder and parked his upright spinner suitcase against the wall. Toby said he hadn't made much use of this place in a year, which explained its dank smell. Brian crossed the room and opened the windows to let out the musty air.

Glancing around, he rubbed his palms together. So...what should he do first? A swim in the lake? Brian considered it, but his gaze landed on the white refrigerator. On second thought, he'd better get to town and pick up some groceries.

Decision made, he left the cabin, climbed into his truck, and drove back to the highway in search of the nearest grocery store.

❦

"I dropped off the rest of the apple pies at the Foodliner."

Talia Fountain gazed up from the shelf she'd been stocking and smiled at her mother.

"Sure was nice of Jim Graves to agree to sell our day-old pies. Of course," Mom added with a grin, "they are the best in the world, if I do say so myself."

"Of course," Talia agreed. She'd grown up with Mom's fresh-baked apple pies, and twenty-eight years later, she still loved them. Mom continued to bake her fruit-filled desserts each morning, using natural ingredients with no preservatives or chemicals, and they were sought-after commodities in Blossom Lake. Tourists from every state in the Union vacationed here...and looked forward to Marlene Fountain's pies, sold exclusively at Talia's health food store, *Fountain of Life*—and now available at Jim's Foodliner too.

"I think you made a wise decision, letting Jim sell our leftover bakery," Mom said. "It might persuade some of his customers to stop into your store for their vitamins and herbal supplements."

"That was my thinking exactly."

Talia stood and stretched the kink from her back. She'd been dusting and arranging the lower shelf for the past forty-five minutes. Facing shelves was a task that seemed unending, and more so depending on the volume of customers. She rejoiced that the number was increasing. Talia had only been in business for a little more than twelve months, but was nearly forced to close, what with last year's slow winter season. Fortunately, sales had picked up after the Memorial Day weekend—a direct answer to Talia's prayers.

She glanced around her store lined with shelves. Her father had built each unit to fit the old walls, something of a feat as the building was over one hundred and thirty years old.

She smiled. Talia loved this old place. Sometimes, she imagined what they'd say if walls could talk. What a history they'd experienced over the last century. From horses and buggies to high-speed sports cars, these cracked plaster walls had witnessed it all.

"Talia, are you daydreaming?"

"No." With a blink, she snapped from her musings.

Mom chuckled lightly. "I see that guilty grin." She rolled her eyes. "You can't hide anything from your mother, you know."

"I know," Talia muttered.

Mom smacked her hands together. "What else do you want me to do?"

As Talia pondered the question, she marveled at Mom's healthy appearance. Her legs were tan and shapely in navy blue walking shorts, evidence of their daily jogs, and Mom's red, white, and blue striped T-shirt hugged her figure better than anything Talia wore. Mom's enviable blonde hair hung loosely to her slender shoulders, and her German peaches-and-cream complexion was an example of good eating habits, sunshine, fresh air, and exercise. At sixty-three years old, Marlene Fountain didn't look a day over fifty. She was, in fact, the one who influenced Talia to pursue a career as a dietician, now turned health food store entrepreneur.

"A shipment of vitamins came in this morning," Talia said in reply to her mother's inquiry. "Want to unload boxes?"

"Sure."

Mom strode to the back of the store, and Talia smiled in her wake. She felt so fortunate to experience a close relationship with her mother.

*Thank you, God,* she silently prayed, *that Mom is my friend—and an employee who doesn't expect a paycheck.*

Talia probably would have given up her business out of sheer discouragement this past year if it hadn't been for Mom's support and Dad's financial advice. She'd been blessed with Christian parents who not only longed for her to succeed financially, but desired for her store to flourish and glorify the Lord as well.

*And I pray it does, Lord Jesus,* Talia whispered, stooping to resume her duties of facing and dusting the next shelf up from the bottom.

The tinkling of the tiny brass bell on the door signaled a customer's entrance. Talia glanced over her shoulder in time to see Dirk Butterfield strut in wearing an expensive-looking gray suit and coordinating silk tie.

Talia willed away the scowl pinching her brows. The man was all pomp and circumstance and enjoyed telling folks of his position on the town board. But worse, Butterfield's good friend owned a national drugstore chain, and he would love to see *The Fountain of Life* go out of business. That way, the big box store could move in and supply this town with its brand of vitamins and health products. Butterfield was pushing for this entire historic corner of shops, one of which Talia rented, to be demolished and replaced with one of those enormous super centers, identical in every city. In fact, a town hall meeting was scheduled for September on the very subject, but Talia felt confident that she and the other shop owners would prevail. Dirk Butterfield wasn't going to rob her of her success, that's for sure. If she could battle and overcome her discouragement to keep her business, she could fight with everything in her to keep her doors open in this prime location.

However, the fact that Butterfield had entered *Fountain of Life* meant trouble.

Slowly, Talia stood. "Good afternoon, Mr. Butterfield," she said with feigned politeness.

"Afternoon." He eyed her inventory and floor space with a critical expression. "Not many customers today, eh?"

"You just missed the rush," Talia quipped.

Butterfield gave her a condescending grin. "My wife asked me to pick up some concoction. She tells me it's supposed to alleviate allergy symptoms."

Talia grew wary. The man wanted to spend money at *her* store? Surely not. Maybe this was a trick. She'd best proceed with caution, although she couldn't resist showing off a bit of her knowledge of herbal remedies.

"I think Mrs. Butterfield might be referring to this..." Talia led the well-dressed man toward the back of the store. "This allergy relief tea. It can be sipped hot or cold." Talia handed the product to him.

"What's in it?" He inspected the box.

"Ginger and licorice root, eucalyptus and orange peel...the ingredients are listed on the package."

"Hmm..." Butterfield furrowed his auburn brows. "And you guarantee this product will take away my wife's sneezing and watery eyes?"

Talia placed her hands on her hips. "I make the same guarantees that medical doctors make." She tipped her head. "Have you ever heard physicians guarantee their cures, invasive or otherwise? They don't. They can't. And neither can I. So, my suggestion is that you tell your wife to sample the herbal remedy and see if it helps. It's been known to help millions of others."

Butterfield handed back the box of tea. "Don't you carry something in pill form? That would be much more convenient."

"Sure." Replacing the tea, Talia stepped to the next shelf. "Mrs. Butterfield can try this." She handed him four white plastic bottles with blue and white label. "I recommend a combination of alfalfa, vitamin C, garlic, and zinc."

"All of that?" The man brought his chin back sharply. "I can go find a drugstore and buy an antihistamine/decongestant, and then my wife would only take *one pill*."

So that's what this game was all about.

She replaced the bottles to the shelf and smiled politely. "Yes, you can purchase whatever you'd like. The choice is yours. Now, if you'll excuse me, I have some work to finish up."

"By all means. I'll just browse."

Talia wished he would *just leave* instead. Couldn't he find someone else to pester?

She returned to tidying shelves. Minutes later, she heard the bell on the door. Glancing in that direction, she glimpsed Butterfield's retreating form and sighed with relief.

❧

Brian let the pie melt in his mouth. Man, this stuff was the best. He hadn't eaten apple pie in what seemed like a lifetime, so when he found it on sale at the Foodliner, he couldn't resist the urge to buy one…make that two. After all, Jesus said man could not live by bread alone, and Brian suspected man would do all right for a long time on these delicious apple treats.

He took another bite. Cinnamon and tart apple flooded his senses. He read the printed wrapper covering the rest of the pie.

"No chemicals or preservatives," it touted. "All natural ingredients." That didn't mean a whole lot to Brian, but what did impress him was the fact that these sweet delights were really homemade. The woman at the checkout said someone named "Mrs. Fountain" baked them daily, and they were sold fresh at her daughter's health food store down the street.

But hey, even a day old, this pie still tasted delicious.

Brian chuckled inwardly and set aside the wrapper. In his opinion, health food stores were rather nonsensical. Sure, herbal inventions helped some of his patients, but in a more psychological way than a physiological one. However, the idea of natural medicines was exploding in popularity. Even so, Brian found no scientific proof that supported the value of vitamins and herbs, so a person may as well ingest the grass and brew tree bark.

Brian ate another forkful of apple deliciousness. No plate needed. He ate right out of the tin. Mmm, talk about prescription-strength stuff. This pie was doing wonders for him. His mom had been a career woman and no culinary expert by any stretch of the imagination. Dad was equally busy, so frozen or boxed dinners were what Brian had grown up on and what sustained him in his adult life—especially after April died. Odd how a kind of hollowness still threatened to suck him in, like a strange dark vacuum of gloom. It had been ten long years since his wife's passing...

His thoughts heavy, Brian walked through the living room area and onto the screen porch. He gazed downhill beyond the forest and to the sparkling lake. He and April had enjoyed a short but intense marriage. Then, only three months after they'd taken their vows, she was diagnosed with ovarian cancer. She was dead less than a year later. But through the awful trial by fire, God had clearly shown Brian that he was to pursue a career in medicine. So, at the age of twenty-five, he enrolled in med school. Now, however, confusion and frustration overrode his determination. He felt like the proverbial doubting wave upon the sea being tossed to and fro.

"Lord Jesus, what do I do?" he murmured. "What do I do?"

His gaze still resting on the serene lake below, he thought of a line his father often used. "When the going gets tough, the tough go fishing."

Brian grinned. Sound advice, indeed.

Making his way back through the cabin, he set the pie tin on the counter and began scrounging for a pole, line, and tackle box. Finding the needed gear some time later, he strode down to the quiet, peaceful lake.

# Two

"THAT RAT STOLE four bottles of my best vitamins and herbs along with a box of herbal tea!" Talia stamped her foot. "Dirk Butterfield makes me so mad!"

Mom quit wagging her head. "Oh, Talia, Dirk Butterfield would never do something like that. He's an upstanding member of our community."

"He's a thief! I'm tempted to call Sam," she said, speaking of Blossom Lake's sheriff.

"Sam will say that if you can't prove it, your suspicions are merely that. Besides, wild accusations will make you pale in comparison to Dirk Butterfield's solid reputation around town. When the board convenes in September, people will remember this incident."

Talia huffed and placed her hands on her hips. "Whose side are you on, Mom?"

"Yours, of course, which is why I'm pointing this out."

"Well, don't think that highfalutin Dirk Butterfield doesn't hope to make a fool of me before the meeting. You're right. That's likely his plan, which is why he stole those items." Talia fumed. "If he ever comes in here again, I'm going to watch him like a hawk."

"I guess that's all you can do for now, although we can report the theft. Just don't mention Butterfield's name."

"But he was the last customer in here yesterday."

"How about if I pay for the missing items and you forget this nonsense?" Mom sighed. "Dirk Butterfield has a lot of money. He can afford to buy them."

"But I'm struggling financially and he wants to hurt me." It was motive enough. But, glimpsing the worried frown that creased Mom's blonde brows, Talia relented. "Perhaps I'll let this go. I'll simply be smarter in the future where Dirk Butterfield is concerned."

"Good idea." Mom nodded.

The bell on the door jangled, and Talia turned to see a man with dark-blond hair enter. He wore blue jeans and a forest green polo shirt that accentuated his hazel eyes. His attractive face, square jaw and straight nose, reminded Talia of a Hollywood film actor. Several movie stars vacationed in Blossom Lake, although she wouldn't recognize one if he or she passed her by on the street. She smiled. Maybe this guy was famous.

She stepped forward. "Hi. Welcome to *Fountain of Life*."

"G'morning." He sported a cheery expression. "I'm looking for the lady who makes those scrumptious apple pies."

"That would be my mother." She turned and presented her. "Marlene Fountain."

"A pleasure to meet you. I'm Brian Coridan." He approached and offered his right hand.

Mom shook it politely.

"I've enjoyed your pies." A hint of a blush crept into his face. "I ate one for dinner last night and finished the other one at breakfast."

"Well, they are rather small," Mom said, always the diplomat. "I'm glad you liked them."

Brian turned to Talia. Taking his proffered hand, she introduced herself.

"So..." His gaze wandered the store. "You're the owner of this place, huh?"

Talia widened her eyes. "Is that so surprising?"

"No, I only meant...well..."

Talia realized he meant no harm. "I apologize for being defensive. We had a..." Dare she call it a theft? "We had *an incident* here yesterday afternoon, and I'm still reeling from it."

"Sorry to hear it."

Mom stood slightly behind Talia and gripped her shoulders. "If your diet consists of only apple pies, Mr. Coridan, you might be interested in purchasing some multivitamins."

He chuckled at the obvious sales tactics. "I'm a medical physician and don't take much stock in vitamins. Thanks anyway. But I will buy another apple pie."

"Coming right up. I've got several on the cooling rack."

Talia watched Mom walk to the kitchen located in the back of the store. Finally, she stared back at her customer. "So you're a handsome doctor, huh?" There. She'd give him a bit of his own smart-alecky medicine.

He shrugged. "Guilty on at least one of those charges." He grinned.

In spite of herself, Talia felt rather—charmed. "You must be new in town."

"You got me again."

A man who could admit she was right? Imagine that. "Where are you from—if you don't mind me asking."

"Not at all. I'm originally from Virginia, but I got accepted to med school in Milwaukee and ended up going into practice in the same vicinity."

"Ah...so you've escaped from the big city."

He chuckled. "I sure did."

*Probably married.* "Well, I hope you and your wife and kids will take advantage of all the recreation that Blossom Lake has to offer."

"Oh, I'm not married. Not anymore."

So he's divorced with a large alimony payment. She folded her arms.

Dr. Cordian's gaze swept over her, and Talia blushed at his open appraisal. Yes, she'd been fishing, but not on the lake. However, he'd find what every other guy did—Talia was just another single plain Jane with a mousy-colored tangle of curls and ordinary brown eyes. She possessed a so-so figure. Nothing special here.

And yes, she was another health food freak. Judging from his statement about multivitamins, it was doubtful that he'd respect her views on natural remedies versus prescription and over-the-counter drugs.

"So who takes care of your husband and kids while you're working?" Dr. Cordian snapped his fingers. "Let me guess. Your mom does, in between baking up all that apple goodness."

*Rude!* Talia clenched her jaw in preparation for giving him a slice of her mind and tossing his pie order at him. But then she caught sight of the teasing glimmer in his eyes. She smiled. If nothing else, Dr. Coridan was clever. "I'm not married. Never was. No kids."

With pursed lips, he gave a nod and clasped his hands behind his back. Without further comment, he began perusing her inventory. "Were you born and raised in Blossom Lake?"

"No. I'm originally from a little town south of here whose name isn't even on the map, it's so tiny. My parents retired here in Blossom Lake and, after college, I decided to join them and go into business for myself."

"I admire the entrepreneurial spirit." He examined the free literature on the black wire spinner-rack near the doorway. "But I can't say I'm fond of this New Age herbs and sprouts stuff."

"Actually, I don't consider the concept of natural wellness to be New Age at all." She moved toward him. "In fact, much of what's on the market today in the way of herbal remedies dates back to biblical times."

"Lots of people died in those days because physicians didn't have the resources we utilize today."

"True, but so much of medicine is profit and gain and putting money into the pockets of executives at insurance and drug companies. It's not, in my opinion, about the welfare of patients."

Brian gave the rack another spin. "I might agree with you there."

"Really?"

He glanced at her and grinned. "Surprised?"

"Yes." But pleasantly so.

Mom reentered the shop carrying an apple pie wrapped in a brown paper sack. "Here ya be." At the cash register, she rang it up.

Dr. Coridan extracted his wallet from his back pocket and paid. "Thanks much." He nodded toward Talia. "Nice meeting you ladies."

"The pleasure was ours," Mom said. "Stop in again."

Watching Dr. Coridan's retreating form, Talia found herself hoping he would do exactly that.

❦

Brian walked slowly down the street. Okay, so he was having a nervous breakdown. Practicing medicine had pushed him beyond the scope of his emotional abilities and he only now experienced its side effects. A post-traumatic response. What else explained these waves of anticipation? He felt like a backup quarterback who'd just gotten his big chance to play, and he wanted to prove to the coach, the team, and to the fans, that he could win the trophy.

But could he?

Brian almost laughed aloud right in the middle of the busy sidewalk. But then, the only thing he would prove is that it really did lose his mind.

Talia Fountain. She certainly captured his attention with her pluck, and she'd fueled his imagination with her smile. If he asked her on a date, would she accept?

Man, but it had been a long time since he'd asked a woman out. For the past ten years, Brian had shied away from most social circles, save for church functions. He never wanted to be in a position where he'd meet single women. He had no intentions of replacing April.

Except, April was now with the Lord.

But maybe he was jumping the gun. A date didn't mean marriage. It meant a hearty, tasty dinner and pleasant conversation. Nothing more.

Shifting the paper-encased pie to his other hand, Brian decided to revisit the idea of asking Talia out later. Right now, his own business at Blossom Lake's City Hall took precedence. Yesterday, a neighbor spotted him out on the water and suggested that Brian obtain a fishing license for the summer. Wouldn't be much fun to get a ticket, the neighbor said, and he then informed Brian that the lakes up here were heavily patrolled. Being a city boy at heart, Brian hadn't any idea, but he was always one to do things the right way. So this morning, as he was in town and City Hall was within walking distance, Brian figured this was as good a time as any to take care of any fishing legalities.

Entering the red brick building, Brian's gaze settled on the smartly dressed man who leaned on the counter and talked to the receptionist. On second thought, the word "flirting" more accurately described it. The man's head of thick auburn hair tilted ever so slightly as he droned on about the expensive sports car he'd recently purchased. The petite blonde in a red dress on the other side of the desk didn't look a day older than twenty-one.

"Oh, Dirk," she crooned on an excited note, "you'll have to take me for a ride."

"You got it, babe." Spotting Brian, he straightened. He looked guilty, like a naughty child—or maybe like a married man.

Talk about a stereotype. Brian had him pegged, and his assessments weren't usually wrong. Regardless, he nodded a curt greeting to the guy.

"Oh!" The receptionist donned her professional face. "I didn't see you there, sir. What can I do for you?"

Brian stepped forward. "I'd like to purchase a fishing license."

"Sure, I can help you with that." She reached beneath the counter and pulled out a form. "Just fill out this section," she instructed while sliding an ink pen toward him.

Brian set to the task. Name, address, phone number...

"I see you found our local health food store," the other man said.

"I beg your pardon?"

The guy chuckled. "The Fountains are the only people I know who package their pies in brown paper bags."

"Oh." Brian glanced at the apple pie on the counter beside him. "Right."

"Dirk Butterfield." He extended his hand.

"Brian Coridan." He gave Butterfield's proffered hand a shake.

"On vacation or are you mixing business with a little pleasure?"

"Vacation," Brian answered.

"Hmm…well, if you like it up here, there's land still for sale." He grinned, displaying large, white, even teeth. "I run the biggest real estate firm in the county. Let me give you my business card."

Taking it, Brian gave it a once over before slipping it into the pocket of his blue jeans. "Thanks."

"Anytime." Butterfield leaned his elbow on the counter. "Now, lemme give you some advice, if I might. Stay out of that health food place. The lady who owns it is a wacko, and the concoctions she sells are nothing but pulverized lawnmower shavings sold in capsule form."

Brian smirked at the lawnmower bit. "She didn't seem wacky to me, and her mother's apple pies are delicious."

"I'll agree with you there," Butterfield said.

"I used to buy my vitamins at *Fountain of Life*," the little blonde behind the counter said. "But then Dirk made me realize how much money I was wasting. I mean, they sell the same thing at the drugstore on the other side of town—and for a better price."

Brian gave the young lady a patient smile and looked over at Butterfield in time to see his patronizing grin.

"Judy has the gift of gab," Butterfield remarked, turning to Brian. "She's got the perfect job. Gabbing all day long."

"Oh, Dirk." Rolling cosmetically enhanced eyes, she laughed.

Brian returned his attention to his fishing license application. After paying the fee, he quickly excused himself. He didn't have a real good feeling about Dirk Butterfield and felt downright sorry for Judy if she was falling for him. Brian had seen the gold wedding ring on the guy's left hand. If he was indeed a married man, Dirk Butterfield's behavior with Judy was grossly inappropriate. Marriage vows were something for which Brian had a high regard. It irked him when he saw people tread on the sanctity of that union.

But it was none of his business.

He reached his parked truck, unlocked the door, placed the pie inside, and climbed in. He came to Blossom Lake to rest and sort out the details of his life. He refused to get involved in anyone's personal affairs.

But did "anyone" include Talia Fountain?

# *Three*

ON SUNDAY MORNING, Brian dressed for church, selecting a pair of navy casual slacks and a light blue-collared shirt. Knotting a coordinating tie, he wondered if Talia was a Christian. He narrowed his gaze at his reflection. Why couldn't he quit thinking about her?

Yesterday, while fishing, the memory of her brown eyes, shining like topaz, flittered across his mind. The gentle ripples in the lake reminded him of Talia's wavy hair, and he found himself imagining how soft it would feel beneath his fingertips. Thoughts of her had crept in far too often in the past forty-eight hours. It also troubled him because this uncharacteristic preoccupation overshadowed his memories of April.

"You've only met her once, you idiot," Brian told the man who stared back at him from inside the mirror. "That hardly constitutes your odd behavior lately." He squared his shoulders. "Get yourself together, Coridan, or you'll be late for service."

Taking his own advice, Brian grabbed his Bible and left the small cabin for Fairway Christian Church. He'd found it in the phone book last night—right above the listing for Talia's store, *Fountain of Life.*

He groaned. Yes, his hold on sanity was slipping. Might as well go farther out on a limb and visit a church he knew nothing about.

As he drove down the stony road to the highway, the brilliance of the morning sunshine made his spirit soar. Window down, he breathed deeply, filling his lungs with fresh air. Blossom Lake on this glorious summer morning, with its tall pines and crystal-clear water, was like a refreshing dose of Heaven. He whistled along with the Christian radio station he'd tuned into. "Joyful, Joyful, We Adore Thee..."

At last, Brian arrived at the country chapel. White window frames complimented the church's blue exterior, and its alabaster-colored steeple reached high into the sky as puffy clouds floated gracefully by. What a great day to be alive.

He strode to the front door and entered a narrow vestibule. His foot faltered as he neared the sanctuary. His pulse raced. There, before his eyes, stood Talia Fountain, handing out bulletins. Wearing a long, printed skirt and short-sleeved green sweater, she looked even lovelier than he remembered.

*Don't hyperventilate.* Was he a teenager or a seasoned physician?

The latter. Brian collected his wits.

Talia spotted him and smiled, and he glimpsed that sweet dimple in her left cheek. "Well, Dr. Coridan, how nice to see you again."

The fact that she recalled his name gave him a thrill. He accepted the bulletin she offered him and nodded cordially, seeing as his mouth went dry of any intellectual uttering.

"Make yourself comfortable anywhere," Talia said. "We're very informal here. No assigned seats or anything, although I must admit people at Fairway tend to park themselves in the same pews week after week." She winked. "How about rocking their worlds a little?"

"Thanks, but I might get seasick." When she didn't laugh, he added. "Rocking? Seasick."

That made her smile. "I've got remedies in my store for that."

"I'll keep it in mind." Was it getting hot in here? He loosened his necktie.

"Forgive my teasing, Dr. Coridan. And seriously, feel free to sit anywhere. You're most welcome here."

"Thanks."

He forced his legs forward. He nearly tripped over a handbag strap sticking out into the aisle. The little blonde who'd sold him his fishing license snatched it up before calamity struck.

"Sorry about that." She scooted over with a silent invitation. "Catch anything yet?"

"Nothing noteworthy."

"Keep trying," Judy advised. "My brother caught a two-foot salmon last weekend."

Brian grinned. "That's not one of those infamous fish stories, is it?"

"Fish story?" Judy blinked, looking puzzled. "We are talking about those things that swim in the lake, right?"

"Right." He chuckled. "Never mind. I'm not a good comedian. Have a good day."

"Sure. You too." She gave him a wary glance as he passed.

Way to resemble a total fool. His levity wasn't going over well this morning.

Brian made his way farther up the center aisle and randomly selected a pew. He sat at its end and opened the bulletin. He read that volunteers were needed to help grill hamburgers and hotdogs at the annual Fourth of July picnic. Would Talia would be there? Would she insist on eating veggie burgers?

*Stop thinking about her, you nut!* But maybe he ought to ask Talia to suggest some herbal remedy that would put him out of his misery.

Maybe he should just ask her out. Period.

"Oh, look, Frank, there's that man I told you about. The one who's been living off my apple pies."

Brian glanced up in time to see Marlene Fountain slide into the pew in front of him.

"Nice to see you, Doctor." She flashed a smile as bright as the sunshine streaming through the impressive stained glass windows. "Talia told us you were here."

"She did?" Was that good?

"This is my husband, Frank." Mrs. Fountain gazed at the man beside her. "This is Dr. Coridan."

He swiveled around the polished oak pew and met Brian's gaze. "Nice meetin' you, Doc." The man's voice sounded like a natural bullhorn.

"A pleasure to meet you too, Mr. Fountain."

"Call me Frank." With his head full of craggy white hair, he resembled a mad scientist. Either that or one of Brian's favorite professors in med school. Brian couldn't decide which.

He shook Frank's beefy hand.

"Nice day, ain't it?"

"Sure is."

A small ensemble, consisting of an organist, a pianist, and a guitarist, began to play near the altar. Frank turned and settled in beside his wife. Moments later, Talia joined her parents.

Great. How would he concentrate on the sermon with her sitting in front of him, swinging those soft curls? Then again, one of the fruits of the Spirit was self-control.

The song ended on a long note, and the music stopped. A casually dressed pastor walked to the pulpit and bid his congregation welcome.

"And now for our announcements." The balding reverend nodded in the Fountains' direction. "Go ahead, Frank."

Talia's father stood, a towering hulk of a man. Without the aid of a microphone, he belted out one announcement after the other, intermittently looking at the bulletin in his hand.

"And we need volunteers to barbecue at our picnic in two days. Who's man enough for the job?"

Brian chuckled under his breath. If that didn't get a few hands raised...

"Hey, Doc, what about you?"

He felt himself pale. "Me?"

"Can you flip burgers?"

He shrugged. Sure, he knew how to cook on a grill, but he had no idea who these people were.

Talia's hand went up. "Can I volunteer, Dad? I might be a female, but I can flip burgers as well as any guy in this church."

Brian grinned at the challenge.

"I dunno, Tal—"

"I'll flip burgers if Talia does." Had those words actually departed through his lips?

"You're on, Doc." Frank smiled. "I'll man the third grill." He looked over his shoulder at the pastor. "Guess that'll do it."

"Amen!" The pastor seemed pleased. "And welcome to our visitor."

Frank stood again. "Sorry. I should have made introductions. This is Doc Coridan. He's visiting Blossom Lake."

"Welcome," came the collective response.

Brian loosened his tie a little more.

Talia turned and smiled at him, and his heart did a perfect somersault.

He smiled back.

*What am I doing?* He'd come up here for peace and solitude, not to go crazy over some woman and grill food at her church's picnic. He had to get a hold of his thoughts. Relax. Breathe.

"Turn your Bibles to Isaiah fifty-five," the reverend said. "This morning's reading is verses eight and nine. 'For My thoughts are not your thoughts, nor are your ways My ways, says the Lord...'"

Suddenly, Brian felt doomed.

# Four

AFTER CHURCH, TALIA exited the pew and began making her way toward the vestibule. Pastor Leland stood at the doorway, bidding church members a good day and shaking hands. She could see Dr. Coridan's sandy-blond hair and broad shoulders two people ahead of her. Talia hoped she'd get a chance to talk with him before he left, although she couldn't imagine what she'd say. See you at the grills on the Fourth?

She felt both flattered and confused by the conditions of his volunteering to flip burgers at the picnic. What did he mean by it? Was he interested in her personally or had he felt it unfair that Dad balked when she'd volunteered? But maybe the good doctor was an expert with charcoal and lighter fluid and wanted to show off. He couldn't be possibly have a romantic interest in her, could he?

Talia vividly recalled the way Dr. Coridan's eyes seemed to caress her every feature when they'd first met. She tried to discount the memory, but it wouldn't go away.

"Well, good morning, Talia." Pastor Leland tanned features turned upward with his large grin. "How's business?"

"Picking up. Thank you."

"That's answered prayer."

Talia smiled. "It certainly is."

After shaking the older man's hand, Talia strode into the tiny foyer. She spotted Judy McEnvoy standing to the side, waiting for the rest of her family.

"Hi, Judy."

The young lady nodded curtly, and as no invitation for small talk was forthcoming, Talia walked past. She made a quick stop in the restroom, pausing for a long moment and scrutinizing her reflection. As always, her curly hair sprang out in every direction thanks to the summer humidity. Perhaps she should have braided it...well, too late now.

Exiting the ladies' room, she passed Judy who averted her gaze this time. Had she done something to offend the other woman? Talia followed her back into the restroom, but then Judy locked herself inside a stall.

"Are you okay, Judy?"

"Of course. Why wouldn't I?"

"Not sure, but—"

The commode flushed, and Talia gave up. Obviously, this wasn't the best time to chat. Whatever bothered Judy would hopefully blow over.

Talia left the church building and walked through the rapidly emptying parking lot. She focused on her dad's car up ahead and spotted her parents standing beside it, conversing with Dr. Coridan.

*He's still here.* She quickened her steps. Perhaps she'd get to talk to him after all.

❦

Brian saw her coming and smiled. He thought Talia looked like a breath of fresh air—if such a thing could be captured in the visual sense. She had a natural, healthy glow in her complexion, and her brown eyes sparkled as she returned his smile.

"Hey, Doc, did you just hear anything I said?"

Brian tore his gaze from Talia, feeling embarrassed. "Um...sorry. What were you saying?"

Frank glanced at his daughter then looked back at Brian. "Just wondering if you'd like to join us for brunch this morning, seein' as you were asking about restaurants in the area."

"I'd enjoy that. Thanks for the offer." Brian hoped Talia planned to go along.

"Every Sunday, we go to Blossoms' Boat House for an all-you-can-eat buffet," Marlene put in. "But they only serve till one o'clock, so we'd best get moving. I'd hate to gulp simply because the place is closing."

"I'll follow you there," Brian said.

He glanced at Talia and she gave him a smile.

On the way to the restaurant, Brian fought with his emotions. He considered himself to be a practical man, principled and skilled. He rarely gave in to his feelings, knowing there was little room for sentiments in the medical field. He would be sobbing every day over his patients' illnesses if he allowed himself such a luxury. And they'd be calling him at home after hours and on the weekends if they ever discovered how much he cared.

And maybe that was his problem. He cared.

Brian slowed at an intersection and trailed Frank in a left turn followed by a sharp right into the restaurant's parking lot. It appeared crowded, and Brian might have been deterred if he hadn't already agreed to join the Fountains for a meal. Truth be told, Brian wouldn't have consented to this little excursion if he didn't think he'd get a chance to get to know Talia better.

No harm in that, right? Getting to know her? Besides, maybe he'd decide they weren't compatible. After all, they held very different philosophies on health care, or so it appeared.

Brian tried to convince himself of that, but when he found Talia waiting at the door for him, all reason took flight.

"Mom and Dad are being seated," she explained. "We have reservations, and it looks like we're going to eat on the back deck. I hope you don't mind eating outside."

"Um...no. That's fine."

Talia reached for the handle on the glass door. "Well, c'mon then." She chuckled lightly before waving him inside.

Brian felt like a fool for the umpteenth time. And a rude one on top of it. Where were his manners? He should have opened the door for her.

He caught her elbow in the restaurant's lobby. She swung around and faced him, her brows arched expectantly. He longed to explain his situation, that he hadn't been on a date in almost twelve years, and that he behaved awkwardly and stupidly. Would she understand or would she scoff?

"Don't be nervous around my parents and me," Talia said as if divining his thoughts. "I realize it can be uncomfortable, meeting new people. I mean, here you are in Blossom Lake, not knowing a soul in town." She smiled warmly, melting Brian's insecurities. "We're just everyday country folks. We don't put on airs. What you see is what you get with us."

With another dimpled smile, she led him to the back of the restaurant and onto the outer deck that was lined with tables.

"I hope we don't disappoint you, Dr. Coridan."

"Brian."

"Brian." She smiled. "You're from the city and probably used to fancier things and more sophisticated people."

"On the contrary. I'm enjoying my stay in Blossom Lake and meeting you...you rural-hearted folks has been great so far."

Talia grinned as they reached her parents. She obviously wasn't such a backward country girl that she didn't pick up on his attraction.

Remembering his manners this time, Brian held the chair for Talia before taking the adjacent seat at the large, square table.

"So what kind of a doctor are you?" Frank inquired as the waitress set two carafes of coffee on the table. One was labeled decaf and the other, regular.

"I'm a family practice physician and I work in a multi-specialty clinic."

"Oh, good. I need some free advice."

"Dad." Talia gave him a scowl.

"Well, docs are expensive," he retorted, "and my insurance doesn't pay much."

Brian grinned at the man's candor. "What sort of problem are you having, Mr. Fountain?"

He raised his arms and hung his head back. "Doctor, Doctor, it hurts when I do this."

"Don't bite, Brian." Talia rolled her eyes. "My dad is the king of obnoxious jokes."

Brian had met the guy less than two hours ago, but he'd already figured Frank was the prankster-type. "My advice, Mr. Fountain, is...don't do that."

"Oh, you two aren't any fun." He righted himself in the chair.

Marlene gave her husband a hooded glance. "Pour me some coffee, dear."

He grumbled but did her bidding. For all the world, Frank resembled a little boy whose prank wasn't appreciated.

Marlene turned to Brian. "Are you visiting family up here?"

"No, I'm renting a friend's cabin for the summer." Brian waited for the coffee carafe then filled Talia's cup before his own.

Frank let out a long, slow whistle. "That's lots of vacation time, ain't it? What about your patients?"

"They're in good hands. The other family physicians are absorbing my caseload. And I might lose a few patients to other doctors, but I really needed the time away." He sipped his steaming brew. "I guess you could say I'm taking a sabbatical from the medical field."

"You don't like being a doctor?" Talia asked.

"Yes, I do. That's not it. It's the politics that goes with the profession that bother me."

"Tell me a job that doesn't have politics," Frank countered. "Bet you can't. Know why? Because wherever there are self-serving people, you'll find policies and agendas."

"I agree," Brian said.

"Even Talia, being self-employed, can't avoid the political landscape. Why, that weasel, Dirk Butterfield, would love to turn the whole town against her so he can—"

"Shh, Dad, that's enough." Talia placed her hand on his forearm. "I'm sure Brian doesn't want to hear about Blossom Lake's very own soap-opera."

"Guess you're right," Frank's face reddened with obvious chagrin. "Sorry, Doc."

"Quite all right."

"Although," Marlene added, "after a couple of weeks in your cabin alone, you might want to hear what's going on. At that point, we'll tell you."

"Yeah, get the scoop from us first," Frank advised.

Talia shook her head at her parents. "You guys..."

The waitress appeared and took their orders—the breakfast buffet all around. Standing, they re-entered the restaurant and Brian noticed the décor for the first time. The tables were a collection of old, wooden country kitchen sets, dating back to the early 1900s. None had been refinished as far as Brian could tell, which made them seem all the more charming. On the walls hung all kinds of fishing and boating paraphernalia, from nets to anchors to rods and reels to propellers and oars. There was even a full-scale rowboat on display, its hull fastened to one large wall in the main dining room.

"Interesting place," Brian remarked, standing behind Talia in the queue at the buffet.

"This building was once an old warehouse."

"I assumed as much."

"What gave it away, the lofty ceiling or the scarred wooden floors?"

"Both, I guess." Brian smiled.

He watched as Talia selected several pieces of fresh fruit. "I love antiquated buildings. They're one of my many passions. So I get a kick out of coming here." She set a bagel on her plate and moved to the scrambled eggs, dishing up a spoonful. "Just north of here, there used to be a logging camp back in the late eighteen hundreds. The men would stack wood on flatbed railroad cars and it was transported here and all over the state."

"I always thought loggers used rivers to move wood."

Talia paused. "Beats me. I'm no historian. I'm simply a champion of historical places."

Brian chuckled and helped himself to the eggs. Out of the corner of his eye, he saw Talia take two sausage links.

"Don't eat the bacon," she whispered.

"Why not?" he whispered back.

"It's got nitrites in it."

"All meat has nitrites in it."

"No, just processed meat, like bologna and hotdogs. But the sausage here is fresh. I asked the cook."

"Nitrites don't hurt you. The Food and Drug Administration wouldn't allow the preservative on the market if it were harmful."

Talia gave him a hard stare. "You trust the government with your health?" She gave a wag of her head. "I certainly don't. Talk about politics!"

"I'll take my chances," he said, selecting two strips of bacon. "I'd rather eat preservatives than rancid meat."

"The choice is yours, of course."

Brian grew uneasy. The health food evangelist in her was emerging and he didn't like it. They'd just finished a very polite debate, but as soon as they became better acquainted, they'd most likely be arguing one philosophy against another. They weren't suited at all.

Heaping fried potatoes onto his plate, Brian sighed with relief. Maybe after breakfast, he could return to his cabin and finally push Talia Fountain from his thoughts for good.

# *Five*

TALIA ATE SLOWLY while listening to Brian answer Dad's many questions. When she learned Brian was a widower, heard the pain in his voice as he spoke of his loss, her heart broke for him. He seemed too young to lose his wife to cancer, although Talia was aware that death didn't respect age. Nevertheless, she thought it tragic that Brian and his beloved had only been married a short while before she died. On the other hand, Brian said his deceased wife had been a believer, so there was comfort in that knowledge. In addition, God had used Brian's wife's death to lead him into the medical field so he could help others.

It was a shame, however, that he didn't believe nitrites were carcinogens. How could he possibly think he helped his patients if he didn't warn them about the food they ate? Talia bristled just thinking about how uninformed most physicians were these days.

"Well, Doc, it was a pleasure meetin' ya," Dad said after they'd finished their meal and now stood in the parking lot.

"Same here."

The two men shook hands.

"I hope I didn't bore you by talking about myself."

"Nonsense. You'll find you've got friends in us, Doc."

Brian smiled. His gaze touched on Talia, although briefly. Was he embarrassed for sharing details about his wife's death and of the aggravation he experienced with his medical practice? There was no shame in it. In fact, Talia enjoyed getting to know him better.

"Oh, and about the Fourth," Dad added, "meet us at the park. You can't miss it. It's right off the highway, across from the grocery store."

"I've seen it," Brian replied. "And I'll be there."

He nodded a farewell to Marlene, and then to Talia, who felt disappointed at the impersonal goodbye. She'd thought for certain that Brian was interested in her. Wasn't he going to ask her out...or at least request her phone number?

Maybe he didn't want to ask in front of her parents. And he knew where to find her. Although it was possible that her mind worked overtime and she only imagined Brian's interest.

Talia climbed into the backseat of the car. Dad and Mom slid into the front, Dad behind the wheel.

"I'm going to marry you off yet." Dad glanced at Talia through the rearview mirror.

"What do you mean?"

"That doctor's got eyes for you, that's what I mean."

Talia didn't reply. Instead, she pondered the idea. So her father had gotten the same impression.

"I thought the same thing, Tal," Mom said, "from the minute Dr. Coridan entered your store."

"Well, he might have been interested," Talia agreed, "at first. But I don't think he is anymore."

"Why do you say that, honey?" Mom turned as far as the seatbelt allowed.

"For one thing, our beliefs about health care are at opposite ends of the spectrum. For another..." Talia sat forward. "We barely know this guy. We might know more about him now, but don't you think it's a wee bit early to start thinking about a wedding, Dad?"

"Now, Tal, I'm being open-minded. Isn't that what you and your sisters wanted all these years? An open-minded father?"

The man was impossible. "That was when we were teenagers and wanted the car. It's too late for open-mindedness now." She laughed. "We have our own vehicles."

"I can't win," he muttered.

Talia laughed at her father's favorite line. He'd used it for the past twenty-five years, maintaining it wasn't easy living in a household of females. As the youngest of three girls, Talia figured she'd caused him the most grief. Her sisters finished high school, had gotten married, and gave birth to four kids between them. They led decent, quiet lives, owned homes, and were devoted to their families. Nothing wrong with that—in fact, Talia often wished she had a similar lifestyle. Unfortunately, Mr. Right just never seemed to come along and sweep her off her feet.

Dad said she was asking for too much. He told her, "Real men don't sweep. You need to start thinkin' practical."

*Practical.* Talia wasn't wired that way. She was a dreamer, and the more people urged her into sensibility, the more she longed to chase her dreams.

Her first of many came true when she opened *Fountain of Life.*

Her second included a man who would sweep her off her feet and share in her entrepreneurial aspirations. But since Talia didn't consider herself a raving beauty, she figured Mr. Right would have cataracts, or better yet, proverbial stars in his eyes. In other words, love would, indeed, have to be blind.

But that hardly described Dr. Brian Coridan. Instead, the words handsome, sophisticated, with eyes wide open more accurately applied to him. He was a man accustomed to city life. What could he possibly see in a plain bumpkin like herself—a bumpkin with an attitude, at that? A bumpkin with opinions about health care that vastly differed from his own.

No—if Brian held the slightest bit of interest in her prior to today, it passed with this morning's brunch.

❧

"Glad you made it, Doc!"

Brian strode toward Frank Fountain and pushed out a polite grin. "I'm a man of my word."

"So I see."

"Hope I'm not late." He didn't want to be here at all. In fact, it took every ounce of energy he possessed just to show up today. The last thing he wanted to do was foster any false hopes that Talia might harbor.

But that didn't stop him from thinking about her.

"Nope. That grill over there is waitin' on you. Coals are nice and hot."

Brian gave a nod and chanced a look at Talia. She'd dressed in festive attire, a long skirt printed in red, white, and blue, and a navy T-shirt. But she didn't so much as glance at him and appeared to concentrate on the food she cooked over smoky flames. Brian wondered why he felt...jilted. And yet, wasn't disinterest the effect he desired? He hadn't bothered to seek her out since their Sunday brunch.

"Grab yourself a pair of them plastic gloves. Then take up a plate of meat and slap the burgers on the grill."

Brian did as Frank instructed. Wearing protective clothing wasn't new to him. Once on, he took up the plate of raw hamburgers and hotdogs from off the picnic table. Doing so, he noticed the red and white checked cloth and the potato salads, baked beans, pies, and pans of chocolate brownies on display.

"Sure is a lot of food over there," Brian remarked as he returned to the smoking grill.

"Yep, and there'll be more after we're done cooking up these dogs and burgers. Folks will be expecting to eat at noon...sharp."

Brian didn't waste another moment and focused on his task of turning the meat. Every now and again, he flicked a gaze in Talia's direction but never caught her eye. She seemed engrossed in her duties at the grill. It shouldn't bother him since they had nothing in common, and yet he felt compelled to win her affections.

Must be pride...or maybe the thrill of the chase. Being an outdoorsman, Brian saw the logic behind the latter.

If that was really it.

At long last, all the meat was barbecued to perfection. Everyone gathered around the food. After the pastor prayed, two lines formed on either side of the picnic tables. Brian decided to make a quick stop at the restroom in the pavilion and wash up before eating. Entering the octagon-shaped building, he nearly ran headlong into Talia who was on her way out.

"Whoa! Where's the fire, Dr. Coridan?"

So she was back to calling him *Dr. Coridan*. "Pardon my rush, *Miss Fountain*. I'm in a hurry because...quite honestly, I'm hungry."

She giggled. "Then I shan't detain you a moment longer," she said in a century-old tone.

Brian's defenses crumbled. He smiled.

Talia's gaze flitted over his left shoulder and her brown eyes darkened. The grin slipped from her face. Following her line of vision, Brian spotted an impressive yellow convertible and Judy climbing out of it. The driver was none other than Dirk Butterfield.

The scene didn't look good, not even from Brian's perspective as a newcomer to Blossom Lake.

Brian turned back to Talia. "I think the Blossom Lake soap opera is unfolding before my very eyes."

Wearing a hint of a smile, she looked at him as if gauging his reaction.

"Butterfield is married to someone other than Judy. Is my assessment correct?"

Talia nodded.

"Hm..." Brian glanced over his shoulder in time to see the sports car speed away and Judy heading for the picnic area.

"Is she a believer?"

"I think so."

"Is he?"

"I doubt it, although I suppose he could be."

"And Judy is aware of his marital status?"

"Everyone in town is aware of it."

Brian digested the information, contemplating why he should even care. He was on vacation, not on some investigation.

"I'll keep both of them in prayer." A pat answer, he knew, but the situation warranted a reply. And pray for the pair he would.

"Me, too," Talia said, staring across the park's vast lawn. "But it's hard. I dislike Butterfield." Her expression brightened. "Hey, do you play volleyball?"

"Yes, except I haven't played in about fifteen years."

She smiled. "Then you'll have to join us after lunch. It's a fun time."

"I'll think about it."

"Okay." With a little wave of her hand, Talia left the pavilion.

Brian watched her go, taking note of the attractive way her skirt flowed down over her hips and swung around her ankles with each step. And those high-wedged sandals... Did she plan to play volleyball in that outfit?

Maybe he'd have to hang around and find out.

*Six*

BRIAN WATCHED TALIA kick off her sandals and walk onto the sand of the volleyball court. So she planned to play in that outfit, eh? The other participants, an even number of women and men, wore modest shorts or blue jeans, as he did.

Talia stood a few feet away and he couldn't help inquiring. "Aren't you afraid you'll hurt yourself, playing in a long skirt like that?"

She merely shrugged. "Well, it's not like I'll be running bases or anything. All I have to do is stand here and hit the ball with my fists."

Brian grinned at the quip.

"Talia always wears a skirt," a petite woman on the other side of the net informed him. "She's an odd duck."

"Oh, quiet, you old married lady."

The other woman laughed and glanced adoringly at the man next to her.

Smiling, Talia turned to Brian. "That's one of my best friends, Joellen Patterson. Well, no, it's actually Sullivan now. Joelle and

Todd, the guy beside her, got married six months ago. It was a beautiful Christmas wedding."

Brian was tempted to ask Talia why she'd never gotten married. The answer, however, was obvious—the Lord hadn't brought about the right man for her.

*And I'm sure not the right one.* Brian stepped back and took his place in the last row. At least he'd gotten that much straightened inside his head. She was a health food nut and even her girlfriend called her an "odd duck."

"Hey, Greg," Talia hollered, her hands cupping her mouth, "are we gonna stand here all day or are you gonna serve that ball?"

The dark-haired man in a sleeveless tank top standing in the far corner on the other side of the net gave her a quelling look. "I'll serve. But only if you don't send it back. How's that?"

The ball came flying over the net. The man on Brian's left volleyed it, and a woman beside Talia bumped it back over to the other side where it hit the ground.

"Yes!" With her hands in the air, Talia swayed her hips from side-to-side. "Ha, ha, Greg. You're gonna lose this game."

Brian chuckled at her antics. Talia knew how to keep a game alive, that's for sure.

"Bet you an apple pie we don't." Mischievousness glimmered in Greg's eyes.

"You're on."

The game continued.

Brian played hard while the sun beat down on him and the others. They volleyed, bumped, and spiked the ball back and forth. At one point, Talia's baiting had everyone laughing hysterically, Brian included. He could hardly catch his breath. A ploy to distract Greg, a self-proclaimed volleyball champ. Of course, he earned the brunt of Talia's teasing. After one heroic save, she shouted, "Whoo-hoo, that was great. But this isn't the Olympics, Greg. It's just the Fourth of July."

Everyone burst into laughter, and with Talia to knock him off his high horse every few minutes, Greg seemed to take the game less seriously.

But, after a while, the sparkling blue lake, just several feet away, began inviting Brian to its cool depths. Drenched in perspiration, he wondered if anyone would miss him if he stole away for a swim.

As the idea grew more appealing, one of Greg's female teammates surprised him by dumping a bucket of cold water over his head. The competition stopped and the other players hooted with laughter.

"That's for giving me such a hard time for missing the ball a few minutes ago," the young lady said with a laugh. She tossed her head, her dark ponytail swinging, and strode away.

Even Greg chuckled.

"Water fight!" someone yelled.

Brian made for the lake with the others. It appeared he'd get his swim, after all.

He glimpsed Talia from out of the corner of his eye. He blinked and she was gone. One moment she strode toward the water along with everyone else, and the next she disappeared from his peripheral.

Brian halted and turned back. Talia sat in the sand, her face contorted in obvious pain. Between her hands, she held her right ankle.

⚬⁀⊙

"You okay, Tal?" Joellen knelt beside her in the sand. "That was a nasty spill you took."

"I stepped in someone's archeological dig." Talia winced. "I twisted my ankle."

Brian ventured over. "Can I have a look?"

"I think it's fine." The last thing she wanted was Dr. Brian Coridan's pity. She already felt like the biggest klutz in the world. "This is what I get for teasing Greg during the volleyball game."

"Accidents happen."

Brian hunkered in front of her and cupped her heel in the palm of his hand. His touch was expert yet gentle as he inspected her injury. Already, her ankle had swelled and an ugly bruise had formed.

"It's probably just a bad sprain, but I think you need an x-ray to be sure." He set down her foot with the utmost of care.

"But that means I'll have to go to the hospital." Talia couldn't keep the distress from her tone.

Brian replied with a single nod.

"But it's the Fourth of July."

He gave her a sympathetic grin.

"Want me to get your dad, Tal?" Joelle asked.

She nodded and her friend took off toward the picnic area.

"Let me help you to your feet. See if you can stand." Brian extended his hand.

Taking it, Talia did her best to get to her feet. But the moment she put the slightest bit of weight on her ankle, white lightening-hot pain shot through her head. Then the whole world began to spin.

The next thing Talia knew, she was in Dr. Coridan's strong arms and he was carrying her to her parents' car.

❧

Lying on the hospital bed, Talia couldn't believe her bad luck. Well, actually, she didn't believe in luck. She believed in God.

*Lord, why did You allow this to happen to me?*

She recalled the book of Job and how God took that faithful servant of His through a deep valley of pain and suffering. But in the end, Job had come forth as gold.

But a broken ankle was hardly significant in comparison to what Job experienced.

Talia took a deep breath and willed her anxiety away as she waited for the emergency physician to return. He'd already told her that the x-ray showed a broken bone. He said he would text the orthopedic surgeon on call and find out the next step. Apparently, surgery wasn't out of the question.

Her insides filled with nervous flutters. She'd never undergone surgery before. She'd been a picture of health up to this point. She had taken extra special precautions never to put anything artificial into her body. Glancing up at the IV threaded into her right arm, she wondered what chemicals entered her system in the form of pain medication.

"So how's the patient doing?"

Talia looked over at the curtained doorway. Brian walked in.

She managed a polite smile. "I'm okay. Just a little frightened." Her vision blurred with unshed tears. "On second thought, I'm a lot frightened!"

"Of what?" Brian stood beside her bed. He leaned his tanned forearms on the guardrail and peered down at her.

"I'm afraid of going under the knife." She barely eked out the words. "Not only am I a klutz, but I guess I'm a big baby too."

A smile inched its way across Brian's face. He'd gotten a bit sunburned today. Talia would have to give him some Vitamin E lotion. "It doesn't look like surgery is in your future so you can relax."

"Really?" Her heart swelled with hope.

"That's my diagnosis, anyway. I was with your parents when the ER doctor showed us the x-rays. Oh, and, by the way, your mom and dad said you should call one of their cell phones when you're finished here. They went back to the picnic to clean up."

Talia nodded.

"I told them that I'm happy to give you a lift home and save them a trip back out here."

"That's very kind of you. Thanks." She'd never met a more sensitive man, and she couldn't help but recall the way he'd so effortlessly swooped her up into his arms. "But I hate for your holiday to be ruined on my account."

"It's not ruined. I had more fun today than I've had in years." He straightened then strode to the padded green vinyl chair adjacent to the bed. "Of course, I will expect to be compensated for my time."

Talia turned her head and noted the teasing gleam in his hazel eyes. "Oh? And what do you want? A year's supply of my mother's apple pies?"

"Oooh, I hadn't thought about that." He looked upward, wearing a contemplative smirk. "Here I was thinking of dinner and a movie or something."

*A date?* In spite of herself, Talia smiled. So Dr. Coridan was interested in her, after all. Well, she was rather interested in him too. But could he accept her, with her unique philosophy of medicine along with all her quips and quirks?

"I don't go to movies," she blurted. "But I don't look down on others who do. It's just a personal conviction with me."

"Like always wearing a skirt?"

Talia nodded. "Most people think I'm weirdo—even some of my Christian friends. But God dealt with me on the issue of my immodest clothes when I was in college. Shortly thereafter, God showed me that the movies I loved to watch and the type of music I enjoyed both became idols in my life. They had to go. I obeyed." Gazing down at the sheet that covered her to the waist, she picked at imaginary lint. "But you and I could go to dinner and then to an outdoor concert. A small symphony plays in the park every other Saturday night."

"Sounds nice. I'd like that."

Talia looked at him and glimpsed his curious expression.

"What is it?"

"Nothing."

Talia wondered about the strange light she saw in his eyes. Maybe he wouldn't want to go out with her now that he knew her personal beliefs. But while she wasn't sure what he was thinking, she was glad that he had at least accepted them without criticism.

"You can change your mind and take the apple pies if you'd rather."

Before Brian could respond, the ER physician entered the room. He grinned at Talia. "I spoke with the orthopedic surgeon and faxed him the radiologist's report. It doesn't appear you'll need surgery."

Talia looked at Brian, feeling a bit awed. His diagnosis had been correct. But why should she be surprised?

As if guessing her thoughts, he smiled at her.

"We'll put a cast on your ankle and get you out of here," the ER doctor continued.

"Hallelujah!" Talia's world seemed right again.

# *Seven*

TWO DAYS LATER, Talia sat in the comfy recliner that her father had brought over to the store. Her injured ankle was elevated, and an ice pack lay across the cast in an effort to keep the swelling down. Unfortunately, the pain was nearly intolerable, and Talia wondered why her herbal remedies weren't doing their job.

Mom put her hands on her hips. "Why don't you take one of those pain pills the ER doctor prescribed?"

"Because I don't want more chemicals in my body." Talia was a purist, and Mom knew it. "Who knows what the lasting effects might be?"

"Did you ever think that maybe God gave mankind the ability to manufacture narcotics for such a time as this?"

Talia didn't reply. In truth, she would feel like a hypocrite relying on prescription drugs instead of trusting God and His organic creations to ease her pain.

"Mom, would you mind slicing up a protein bar for me and setting the pieces on a plate near the checkout?" She deliberately changed the subject. "When customers come in, I'll continue being the greeter with the broken ankle, but I can also offer them a taste of the power bars. Maybe we'll generate some sales."

"Certainly. I wouldn't mind in the least." Mom walked to the shelf where she lifted a protein bar from the product box before walking to the kitchen area.

Talia lay back in the recliner and shut her eyes against the overwhelming throb in her ankle. A moment later, she heard the bell on the door signal a customer's arrival. Opening her eyes, she saw Brian enter the shop. In his left hand, he held a bunch of blue wildflowers.

Talia forced a smile through her pain. "Hi."

"Hi, yourself." He strode over to where she sat. His hazel eyes fell over her and paused on her injury. "Nice setup."

"Thanks."

He presented her with the pretty buds.

"How thoughtful of you."

"They're organic. Right from the hill behind the cabin I'm renting. I picked them right before coming here."

Talia wasn't much in the mood for his teasing, so she ignored it. "Thanks, Brian."

He narrowed his gaze. "Ankle bothering you?"

Talia moaned and nodded. "How can you tell?"

"You don't seem like your spunky self, not that I expected you would, considering your injury."

"You're right. Crabby better describes me right now."

"Should I leave?"

Talia shook her head and pushed out a smile. "You're in no danger."

Mom returned with the slices of protein bars and set the plate on a table beside Talia's chair. "Brian, how nice to see you."

"Same here."

"Care to try a natural energy…bad-tasting treat? We're giving away sample bites."

"Mom! I'll never sell them if you present the product that way."

Brian helped himself to a couple of pieces.

Talia softened. "My poor mother has been good enough to put up with me the past couple of days."

"Jewels in my crown, that's for sure," Mom teased before her expression grew serious. "But, Brian, her discomfort could all be avoided if she'd only take her pain pills."

Brian's eyes grew wide. "You're not taking your medication?"

Talia shook her head.

"You're suffering needlessly."

Talia shifted in the recliner, trying to get comfortable. It seemed a hopeless cause. The throbbing in her ankle caused her whole body to hurt.

Brian took her hand. "Take your pain meds, Talia. They'll help you."

She bit back a harsh reply. Why did she have to keep explaining herself?

"She's afraid they might do some permanent damage," Mom said.

"Our bodies are in perfect balance," Talia eked out. "Synthetic drugs are liable to throw off my whole system for months—or even years."

"Then you'll have to grin and bear it, I'm afraid."

Brian stated half of it correctly. Truth to tell, Talia didn't feel at all like grinning. She felt like crying.

"Personally," he continued, "I'd take the pain medication and then worry about my body's balance after my ankle healed up."

"Spoken like a true physician." Seeing the tautness around his mouth and the hurt in his eyes, she instantly regretted her biting remark.

"Well, I should go." Brian gave Mom a parting grin, but only a glance at Talia. "I hope you feel better."

She wanted to stop him, but what would she say?

"Dr. Coridan, can I interest you in an apple pie? It's on the house since you've done so much to help us."

"I think I'll pass for today." His smile was cool and polite. "I'm still full from the Fourth."

"All right, then. Have a nice afternoon."

"You do the same."

After another glance in Talia's direction, he left the store.

Mom clucked her tongue like a hen to one of her chicks. "Where are your manners, Talia Jean Fountain? Of all the things to say, and after he brought you flowers."

Talia swallowed hard, but couldn't contain the burst of tears that sent her gaze swimming. Her hand shook as she swiped the moist emotion from her cheeks. She felt ashamed, but it hadn't been her intent to wound Brian with her sharp tongue. But perhaps a relationship between the two of them wasn't meant to be anyway. They seemed worlds apart.

Gazing at the soft wildflowers she still held, Talia decided she felt just as blue.

❦

She was nuts. That's all there was to it.

Brian strode to his truck. Main Street in Blossom Lake this afternoon was teeming with people, so he'd been forced to park a few blocks away from Talia's store. All the while he walked, he fumed. No wonder she wasn't dating and never married. She probably ran off every eligible guy she met—including him.

Brian halted his wayward thoughts, realizing they stemmed from wounded pride. When he left the cabin earlier, he'd felt like going-a-courtin'. Unfortunately, Talia shot those ideas right out of the sky. Now he wouldn't court that woman if someone paid him.

Except she did break her ankle. If they could swap places, Brian had to admit, he'd likely feel as ornery. But refusing to take her pain meds was foolish.

"Well, well, we meet again."

Brian glanced up before nearly colliding with Dirk Butterfield who stood on the sidewalk no more than a foot away. Brian nodded a polite greeting.

"Judy tells me you're a doctor and that you also play a decent game of volleyball."

"I'll admit to half your statement. I'm a physician." Stepping off to the side so he didn't block traffic on the walkway, Brian grinned. "I can't say I'm a decent volleyball player, although I had fun trying."

He also recalled that Judy had played on the opposing team.

A frown furrowed Butterfield's auburn brows. "Say, how's the little health food store owner? Judy said she'd hurt her ankle."

"She broke it, actually."

"Too bad. That can't be good for business."

"I think her mother helps her out."

"Ah, yes, of course."

Brian glanced around, noting that he stood with Butterfield just outside the man's storefront office. The sign painted on the windows read *Butterfield Realty*.

"So what does a respected medical doctor, like yourself, think of the herbal concoctions that Ms. Fountain sells in her store?"

Butterfield crossed his arms and tipped his head while waiting for a reply.

"I think they're quackery at its finest." Brian couldn't keep the edge out of his voice.

Butterfield chuckled. "I take it you're not a believer in vitamins and herbs?"

He lifted one shoulder in a small shrug. "I'm sure they serve some small purpose, but not to the extent that Ms. Fountain takes it."

"I agree. Say, would you like to step into my office for a glass of iced tea? It's fresh brewed, courtesy of my secretary."

"Thanks, but—"

"Really, Doctor, I can make it worth your while." He shifted his stance. "There's a town hall meeting in September, and one of the topics on the agenda is whether to demolish the corner building that holds those three useless shops." He smirked. "As you may have noticed, they consist of an old-fashioned ice cream parlor, Ms. Fountain's health food store, and that despicable resale shop. I think you can be of some help to me as I'm in favor of the demolition."

Brian lifted a palm to halt the offer. "Mr. Butterfield, I'm here on vacation. I don't want to get involved in Blossom Lake's politics." *Or its dramas.*

"I can certainly understand that." In two smooth moves, Butterfield pulled out his billfold and extracted a wad of bills. He discretely slapped them into Brian's palm. "Give it some thought. An hour of your time is all I ask and, as you'll notice, I'm willing to pay for it."

He turned on his heel.

"Wait!" Brian didn't want the man's money.

Butterfield kept walking and entered his office.

Brian stood staring after him. He glanced at the dollar bills in his hand. He counted it. A thousand bucks. What sort of guy slapped this amount of dough into a stranger's hand?

*The criminal sort.*

Glancing around at the passersby, Brian hoped none of them had seen the transaction. He felt guilty just holding the crisp bills in his palm. He hurried into the realty office, fully intending to return Butterfield's cash.

"Listen, Tal, I'm sure of what I saw."

"Dad, you can't be right."

"Given the way you spoke to Brian minutes ago," Mom said, "it might be true."

Talia stared at her mother. "If he's consorting with the enemy to spite me, then Brian is a very vindictive person, and I don't want a single thing to do with him."

Mom prefaced her reply with a rueful expression. "He seemed like such a nice man..." Her gaze slid to Dad. "Are you sure you saw him take money from Dirk Butterfield?"

"Sure as the sun sets in the west. And after he took the cash, the Doc went inside Butterfield's office."

Talia's heart sank. "I hope Brian understands he's doing business with the devil's spawn."

"Oh, Talia," Mom chided her. "Mr. Butterfield isn't that horrible."

Talia exchanged glances with Dad whose arched brows indicated that he agreed with Talia's remark.

"I s'pose the doc has no way of knowing about Butterfield. We tried to be careful not to gossip at brunch last week."

"True." Mom's expression appeared hopeful. "Let's ask him over for supper tonight and enlighten him. Talia, you can tell him how sorry you are for your snarky behavior."

"Snarky? I don't owe that man an apology." She raised her chin in stubborn opposition. "He's just so full of himself that he can't take a joke."

"Maybe he can't abide a crabby female." Mom's voice was as sharp as Talia's tongue of late.

Another onset of tears clouded her vision. "I'm sorry for being so irritable. As for Brian, if he's involved with Dirk Butterfield in any way, it makes me suspicious. What do we really know about Dr. Brian Coridan anyway?"

"He's a nice guy who cares about you." Mom squinted in silent reprimand. "That's what we know."

"I s'pose I could walk up the street and see if the doc is around." Dad stroked his chin thoughtfully.

"Yes, do that," Mom insisted.

"Stop it, you two. I'm not up for dinner guests."

"But if the doc is a Christian man," Dad said, "and I think he is, then we have the responsibility to warn him about the likes of Butterfield."

"You're right, Frank."

Her parents were testing the last of her patience. "Brian is well-aware of Dirk Butterfield's questionable character. He witnessed Butterfield dropping off Judy at the picnic on the Fourth and he made blatant inquiries which I answered truthfully."

Neither of her folks seemed to be listening.

"Hurry, Frank, see if you can catch up with him."

"Okey dokes." He strode to the door and let himself out of the shop.

Talia looked at her mother. "Maybe I'm going to need a pain pill, after all."

# *Eight*

AFTER BRIAN RETURNED Butterfield's blood money, he continued the trek to his vehicle. He still couldn't believe it. The dude wanted medical information so he could topple Talia's business. Brian wasn't about to get involved in dirty politics, and he refused to share a lick of his knowledge, much to Butterfield's aggravation.

Who needed television? This town had its own homegrown drama.

Brian reached his truck. He unlocked the door with his fob, and he was about to open it when he felt tugging on his elbow.

"Say, Doc, before you go I'd like a word with you."

He recognized Talia's dad's booming voice and turned, smiling. "Sure, but if it's about Talia's ankle, she's got to follow up with her family physician. Not me."

Frank looked somewhat taken aback, and Brian instantly regretted his sharp tone.

"Talia's been hurtin' for the past couple of days."

"Her pain medication will help—if she'd take it."

"I know that, Doc, and you know that, but Talia...well, she's stubborn."

"You don't say." Brian's smile broadened.

"Look, never mind. I thought you were a Christian man. Guess I expected you to act like it. My apologies."

"Don't throw my faith in my face. I'm a Christian, and I try to behave as one ought, but I'm not gullible."

Without a reply, Frank pivoted and walked away, disappearing into the throng of people on the sidewalk.

Climbing into his truck, Brian started the engine. He wasn't about to be manipulated by Frank Fountain...or by anyone else. Talia knew what she needed to do in order to feel better, and he couldn't make her do it.

"Feeling better, honey?"

Back at home and settled onto the sofa in the family room, Talia looked at her mother and nodded. "I hate to admit it, but the prescription drugs worked their magic."

"I told you it would," Dad said from behind his newspaper.

Mom smiled with relief. "I'm glad it helped."

"I'm not!" Unshed tears threatened to choke Talia. "It means I've lived a lie for years."

"How's that?" Dad asked.

"I believed that natural foods, teas, vitamins, and herbs accomplished the same things that prescription drugs did—and better. I was wrong. My business is a sham." She sniffled and swatted at an errant tear.

"Nonsense, Tal." Mom fluffed a pillow and placed it behind her back. "Think of how many people you and your store helped. Remember that woman who came in complaining of migraines?"

"Kathy Krueger."

"Yes, that's the one." Mom took a seat in the upholstered armchair nearby. "You suggested she take at least twelve hundred milligrams of calcium magnesium a day and, what do you know? She followed your advice and hasn't had a headache since. And what about that poor older woman with the chronic insomnia? You sold her a bottle of melatonin and she's sleeping soundly now."

Talia supposed she hadn't been wrong in those instances. "But I couldn't help myself. I studied a dozen textbooks on nutritional tips and healing aids and didn't find a remedy that worked to ease my pain."

Mom gave a sigh. "Perhaps there's a point where God and science meet. That is, God allows the scientists and pharmaceutical companies to discover what He has known from the beginning of time."

"But it's not natural," Talia argued. "It's manmade."

Dad lowered his newspaper. It rustled as he set it in his lap. "This house ain't 'natural' either, Tal. It wasn't here in the woods and I just happened to find it. No, it took a lot of hard work to build by manufacturing companies and machines."

"But that's different."

"How so, dear?" Picking up her knitting, Mom began to work the needles through the colorful yarn.

"This house was built with natural things. Like wood and stone."

"I beg to differ. Brick is manmade, as far as I know," Dad said. "It's manufactured from clay. And what about the insulation and the roof, not to mention the electricity and plumbing? Them pipes didn't magically appear one day."

"All right, all right, you made your point." Talia lazed back against the pillows. "I surrender."

"Hallelujah!" Frank grinned before returning to his paper, and for several long moments, the only sound came from the saw-like buzzing of the cicadas as it wafted through the patio doors.

Talia thought about what her parents said. Maybe today's medical science and the art of nutritional healing could join forces for the good of mankind.

The only question in Talia's mind was…how?

❧

The month of July melted into August's humid heat. The only cure from perspiring discomfort was soaking in the refreshingly tepid lake.

Floating on an inner tube, several feet from shore, Brian closed his eyes and listened to the sounds around him. The twittering birds. The wind rustling trees whose limbs bowed in reverence over the peaceful water. The roar of a motorboat off in the distance. A child's laughter coming from somewhere across the water. These certainly weren't city noises, and Brian wished his time up here wasn't running out. But the truth remained—his sabbatical neared its final stages, and he hadn't made a decision yet about his medical career. He'd assumed that by now, he'd have things figured out.

Worse, he couldn't seem to hear God's voice anymore, speaking to his heart.

When he opened his Bible, the words stared back at him, devoid of their usual depth and meaning. And against his will, a vision of a brown-eyed woman with wavy hair flittered across his mind at the most inconvenient times.

Like now.

Too lazy to fight off any thoughts of Talia Fountain, he let them come. He hadn't seen her in weeks. He avoided going into town and had visited other churches in the area these past Sundays so he didn't run into her. Strange thing was, Brian preferred her church to the others, and he had to admit that he missed catching sight of Talia, whether she was handing out bulletins or playing volleyball. He wondered if her ankle was healing without problems, and then realized that, to his shame, he'd never prayed for her since leaving her store that day.

*Lord, I guess in trying not to think about her, I neglected to pray for her too. But if I lift her up to you now, Jesus, I have to think about her.*

Brian moaned. If he allowed Talia room in his thoughts, she'd slowly make her way to his heart. *Best not to think about her.*

Brian paddled his inner tube toward the shore. He felt like a drowning man, and yet there was no present danger. Instead, it was the sinking feeling that God intended for him to pursue a relationship with the little health food nut, and it was frightening. How would it work? Would it work? They had little in common. But likely, he'd experience little to no peace until he obeyed and followed the promptings of God's Spirit.

Reaching the sandy shoreline, Brian recalled Jesus in the Garden of Gethsemane, praying, "nevertheless, not as I will, but as You will."

Brian felt ashamed of himself. God wasn't asking him to bear the sins of the world and die a cruel death. Rather, he was nudging Brian to emulate Christ in daily life.

He trudged up the hill, dragging the floatation device behind him. He'd been resisting God. No wonder he didn't hear from Him. But swallowing his pride would be difficult, and giving up control of his plans and decisions even harder.

At the cabin, Brian stood on the porch, dripping wet. Spiritually, he was right where God wanted him to be—completely surrendered, and depending on his Heavenly Father.

❧

Cane in hand, Talia limped across the church's vestibule, meeting Judy near the ladies' restroom. She didn't ask if Judy suffered with allergies. Her puffy eyes and red nose answered the unspoken question.

"Hi, Talia."

The greeting surprised her. Talia had fully expected to be snubbed. "Hey, good morning."

Judy tucked her chin and lowered her gaze.

"Are you feeling all right? You look like you might have a sinus thing going on."

"Hay fever."

"Ah..." Made sense. The hay fever season had descended on northern Wisconsin, and already several of Talia's customers had entered the store with allergy-related complaints.

"The allergy tablets from the drugstore make me so drowsy that I feel worse when I take them."

"Well, you're aware of my store's location and what I sell," Talia offered. "Stop by and I'll try to help."

Judy gave her a bland smile. "Thanks."

Stepping closer, Talia peered into the younger woman's face. "Have you been crying?"

Fat tears suddenly filled Judy's eyes. Slowly, she nodded.

"What's wrong?"

Judy shook her head. "I don't want to talk about it."

"Okay, but I'm willing to listen if you change your mind."

Another nod.

Talia wetted her lips. Did Judy's tears have something to do with Dirk Butterfield? It was, perhaps, a lofty presumption, but it warranted addressing. The pair had been spotted around town. "For the record, there's nothing you can say that will shock me. I didn't become a Christian until my sophomore year in college

67

and…well, let's just say that I'm not as naïve as a lot of people might think."

"Thanks."

Judy entered the ladies' room and Talia didn't follow her. She wouldn't push and pry. Instead, she hobbled to the sanctuary. Reaching the center double doors, she glanced around for a place to sit. Her parents sat in their usual pew up front, but Talia didn't feel like limping all the way up the aisle to join them, especially since the service would begin at any moment.

A movement to her right caught her eye and at first, Talia thought it might be Judy. But when she turned, she found Brian standing a few feet away.

Talia was rendered momentarily speechless as their gazes met. But she supposed a simple "hello" would be a good start.

"Hi, Brian."

"Good morning." The grin on his face appeared more wary than warm and friendly.

Talia looked away, although she was always one to wear her heart on her sleeve. "I've been praying you'd come back to church."

When he didn't reply, she peeked at him again.

"I guess it worked—the praying." His smile grew. "How's the ankle?"

"Pretty good. My doctors fitted me with this walking cast." She lifted her foot slightly. "Now I'm more mobile. It's a blessing, because if you think I was a klutz before, you should have seen me on the crutches." She laughed softly. "My father was sure I'd break my neck."

Brian chuckled too, although he sounded more nervous than amused.

Mr. Sanders, one of the ushers, approached them. "Two seats right here in the back row." He pointed out the space. Talia didn't care for the last pew since it was hard to hear the pastor, but she wasn't in any position to be choosey.

Nodding her thanks to the older man, she limped into the sanctuary and scooted into the pew. Brian slid in beside her.

The first song was announced, and when the congregation stood to sing, one more person squeezed into the last pew and claimed a seat on Brian's other side.

It was Judy McEnvoy.

# Nine

TALIA WAS WALKING on clouds—even with a limp in her gait. After the service, Judy asked to speak with her, and the whole sordid story came spilling out. Dirk Butterfield had strung Judy along, making her believe that he would leave his wife and children for her. But then, just days ago, he broke her heart by announcing he'd grown bored with their relationship.

Talia had empathized with Judy's hurt and humiliation. She even shed a few tears of her own. But she was also able to help Judy realize that her pain was a result of sin. Judy accepted her part, confessed it, and begged God for forgiveness. And there it went, her guilt and her shame, as far from the Lord as the East is from the West. However, in Talia's summation, the hardest thing for Judy would be to forgive herself in the days, weeks, and months that followed. Talia promised to help in any way possible and felt so thrilled that God had used her to encourage a sister-in-Christ in this way.

Talia made her way across the sun-baked parking lot and to her parents' car. She spotted them inside, the engine running. The closed windows signaled the use of the air-conditioning.

"Sorry I made you wait so long." Talia climbed into the backseat.

"I'm going to assume it was for a good cause." Dad gave her a speculative glance. "We missed our reservation time at Blossom's Boat House."

"I apologize, but it was a very good cause. But I can't say much more."

Dad backed the car out of its parking spot and drove toward home. All the while, Talia thought about this morning's events and felt a twinge of remorse for not getting a chance to talk with Brian after the service. Judy had claimed her time immediately, and Talia never even said goodbye to him.

Well, the Lord had answered her prayers and brought Brian back to church. The same God of the universe was able to guide Brian back into the store—and back into her life.

⁐

Brian wondered if he was too forward, showing up at Talia's house uninvited this way. He knew where she lived because he drove her home from the hospital on the Fourth of July. But what if the Fountains entertained company this afternoon? It was Sunday, after all, and for some folks, that meant family day. He didn't want to impose.

Thinking about all the "what ifs," Brian nearly turned his truck around, but finally decided to take his chances. He wanted to see Talia badly enough to risk it, although, in retrospect, he didn't know why. Twice now, their opposing philosophies had interfered with opportunities to become better acquainted. Why would this time be any different?

He'd find out the answer out soon enough.

⁐

Talia finished eating lunch and was getting comfortable on the couch with the Sunday newspaper when Mom's announcement perked her right up.

"Brian's here."

"Really?"

Springing from the cushions, Talia limped to the front door in time to see Brian climbing out of his truck. She turned to Mom. "Do I look okay?"

"Adorable."

"Now, hold it," Dad said, coming around the corner. "Not sure I want this guy in my house. He was pretty rude to me the last time I saw him."

"Maybe he came to apologize," Talia said.

"Maybe." Dad's frown deepened. "What about his involvement with Butterfield?"

"Let's ask him about it."

Mom folded her hand around Dan's much larger one. "Your daughter has an answer for everything, sweetie."

"Oh, so now she's *my* daughter, eh?" Dad glowered at her, but all in fun.

Mom kissed him.

"Behave, you two." Talia rolled her eyes.

Brian made his way onto the front porch, and Talia swung open the door. "Hi, Brian. This is a surprise."

"I hope I'm not intruding."

"Not at all. Come in."

"How about a piece of pie and a cup of coffee?" Mom offered.

"Sounds good. Thanks." Brian's gaze flitted to Dad. He stuck out his right hand.

After a moment's hesitation, Dad took it in a polite shake.

"I'm, um, sorry for the way we parted the last time." Sincerity glimmered in his hazel eyes.

Dad conceded a nod. "Me too, especially since I wanted to invite you to dinner."

"More's the pity—for me, that is."

They ambled into the living room, which was decorated in pastels. Dad often referred to it as "the girly room" because of the pinks, blues, and soft greens that incorporated the floral print on the upholstered couch and matching loveseat.

Brian sat on the sofa and Talia took the place next to him. Dad dropped into one of the powder-blue wingback armchairs.

"That day, my dad tried to warn you about getting involved with Dirk Butterfield. He saw the both of you talking and...well, he imagined that Butterfield handed you a wad of cash."

"Which I promptly returned." Brian looked at Dad then back at Talia. "Butterfield tried to pay me for a crash course in medicine. He planned to use any information he gleaned against you and your store at some upcoming town hall meeting."

"That evil scumbag." Talia couldn't help her strong reaction. She'd just heard Judy pour out her heart—the heart that Butterfield shattered with all his lies.

"What's your course of action?" Brian asked.

"He doesn't stand a chance against the other two store owners and me." Talia was convinced of it. "The guy who operates the ice cream parlor printed fliers, and we're handing them out to all our customers. We're expecting a good turnout for our side at the meeting."

"Just to be clear, I didn't give Butterfield any information, but I suspect the guy will find someone else who will." Brian's gaze fixed on Talia. "You might want to be prepared to defend your natural health and healing philosophies."

"I am prepared," she stated confidently, "but the issue isn't my business or the others' either. It's whether the historic building we're renting gets demolished or refurbished."

"True. But from what I gather, Butterfield's angle will be to prove its worthlessness as well as to cite the insignificance of all the shops occupying the old structure. Why keep any of them? That'll be the question he poses to the community."

"Great," Talia drawled.

Brian grinned at her sarcasm.

Mom strode into the room, carrying a tray of slices of apple pie on plates and cups of freshly brewed coffee.

"Looks delicious, Mrs. Fountain." Brian claimed a plate and a cup.

"Do you take cream or sugar in your coffee?"

"No, just black. Thanks."

"You're more than welcome. Frank, will you pray?"

"Isn't dessert covered under the prayer we said at lunchtime?" he groused, but with a teasing gleam in his eyes.

Mom threw an annoyed gaze at him.

"Okay, yes, I'll pray."

All heads bowed in reverence.

"Dearest Lord Jesus, we thank You for this pie and ask that You bless the hands that made it. In Your name, Amen."

"Amen!" came the collective reply.

Talia watched as Brian took a bite of his dessert. "This is the best tasting pie I've ever eaten."

"The secret is the apples." Mom took a plate and cup of coffee and sat in an armchair. "They need to be nice and tart, and I'll have bushels of them in another month or so. We've got a small orchard behind the house."

"Mom makes and freezes the filling," Talia added, "so she can make apple pies all winter long—and they're as pure and fresh as they come."

"My compliments, Mrs. Fountain."

"And as the old cliché goes, 'an apple a day keeps the doctor away...'" Talia could have bitten off her tongue. What a dumb thing to say! She chanced a look at Brian. "I didn't mean *you*. I'm glad you're here now, and I'm sorry I pushed you away weeks ago."

"No worries." Brian grinned before sipping his steaming brew.

Deciding to make light of her blunder, Talia set her fork onto her plate. "Mom, that's what I've been doing wrong!"

"What's that, hon?"

"I've been eating an apple a day. Guess I'd better quit that if I want Dr. Coridan to keep coming around."

Everyone laughed, and any lingering tension evaporated.

❦

Later, after the Sunday evening service, Talia and Brian took a stroll down the gravel road that ran parallel to the Fountains' home. The sun resembled a giant orange fireball as it sank behind the tall pines.

"I'm glad you stopped over this afternoon," Talia said, holding the crook of his arm as she limped along beside him. "Think you can make a habit of it?"

Brian chuckled. "You don't mince words, do you?"

She grinned. "I try not to. I mean, what's the point?"

His smile widened.

"So, when do you leave Blossom Lake and return to your practice?"

"Labor Day."

"Less than a month away."

"I know it, and I'm no closer to discovering God's will for my life than I was when I first came up here."

As they walked on at a slow pace for Talia's sake, she listened to Brian's frustrations. She got the impression that he was too caring a physician to compete in the impersonal world of medicine. He wanted to help people get well, not make money off their infirmities. Doctoring was more to Brian than just a job. It was his livelihood. It gave him a sense of purpose. Medicine to Brian was like ministry to a preacher.

"Sorry," he said at last. "It is wrong of me to dump all that on you."

"You didn't dump. In fact, I'm glad you confided in me. I'll pray for you regarding your decision. It's not an easy one. It will alter the course of your life."

"Right. No pressure or anything." Brian chuckled. "But I suppose the simplest way out would be to do nothing and just accept my present circumstances."

"You don't seem like the kind of man who'd be happy doing that."

"I'd be miserable."

They arrived back at the Fountains' home and sat down on the front porch steps. Talia's ankle throbbed. She winced. "I think I overdid it."

"Some doctor I am." Brian shook his head. The sun had blanched the top of it, making it even blonder. "I didn't give a single thought to your healing ankle."

"You and me both." Talia laughed and stood. "Excuse me for a moment. I need to take a pain pill and the bottle's in the house."

Brian feigned cardiac arrest, his hand over his heart.

"Knock it off, will you? You're as bad as my father."

"You succumbed to pain pills?"

"No other choice than to suffer. It was either that or lose my mind. But you know what I've concluded, Brian?"

"What?" Interest darkened his gaze.

"God calls us to a balance. Too much of anything isn't good, although I still believe people should take control of their health instead of relying solely on doctors."

"I agree."

"But medical doctors serve a purpose too. I learned that fact firsthand on the Fourth of July."

His smile broadened. "Maybe there's a happy medium here, after all."

"Yes, maybe there is."

Brian caught her wrist before she could stand. "Allow me to take the first step, pardon the pun."

Talia frowned, curious.

"There's nothing wrong with my ankle, so how about if I go fetch your prescription for you?"

"How gallant of you." Talia smiled. "Thank you."

# Ten

THE BELL ON the door announced another customer. Looking up from the invoices she totaled at the checkout counter, Talia saw Judy McEnvoy enter the store.

Smiling, she headed straight toward Talia. "That licorice root tea really helped my bronchitis. I slept all night without coughing."

"Glad it helped."

"I also came in to tell you that I've been spreading the word around town about how terrific your store is. I might have damaged its reputation when I was under Dirk's influence."

"Don't worry about it, Judy. The main thing is that it's over and your relationship with the Lord is restored."

"You're very understanding." Judy pushed the blonde hair out of her eyes. "I don't know if I would be so nice if I were you."

Talia rolled one shoulder. "Yes, you would. Forgiveness is what our faith is all about."

"True..."

Talia set her paperwork aside. "Want a glass of iced tea? It's sun tea, and I brewed it this morning."

"Sure."

She went to fetch it, and Judy tagged along.

"My friend Sarah says she saw you and Brian at the park last Saturday night. She said it appeared like you two were having a cozy picnic while the symphony played."

Talia cheeks began to flame, and the late August sun wasn't even bearing down on her. But it was true. They'd enjoyed the coziest of picnics, and the classical music only added to the memorable evening, and they'd seen each other every day for the past few weeks. They talked and got better acquainted during moonlight strolls, outdoor symphonies, and just sitting on the front porch together after dinner. It felt so natural to be with him. She could tell him anything and he'd understand. And, once he'd opened up, Talia discovered that Brian Coridan possessed a heart of gold.

"Brian's a terrific guy." Pouring two glasses of iced tea, she handed one to Judy.

"Uh-oh." Judy frowned. "I see stars in your eyes."

"I'm sure you do." Talia smiled at Judy's astonished expression.

"This sounds serious."

"I wish it were, but he's leaving on Labor Day and returning to his medical practice in Milwaukee."

"There's always email and text messaging, social media. You two can stay in touch."

"Well, that's just it. I'm not sure Brian wants to. He's guarded about his feelings. Keeps a lot inside, unless I pry them out of him." Talia grinned. "He's one of those deep-thinkers."

"Hmm…" Judy sipped her tea.

"But the biggest hindrance in our relationship is the long distance thing. He's not a believer in that old cliché about absence making the heart grow fonder, either. He's communicated that fact. What's more, I agree."

"Bummer."

"No kidding."

"Well, why can't Brian move his practice up here?"

"I'm hoping he'll consider it."

Judy took another swallow of her cold drink. "Why don't you move closer to him?"

"I thought of that too. But my parents are aging, and I wouldn't feel right about moving so far away. Besides, I'm not certain how serious Brian is about me—us. That's one subject I don't want to force."

"I see your point."

"Brian is the kind of guy who likes to make the first move, and that's how it should be. Unfortunately, he's not a man to make a quick decision, and that has its benefits. Once he decides, he's certain. But it has its drawbacks too—like testing my patience."

Judy giggled.

Talia sipped her tea. "Sometimes a future for us as a couple seems hopeless. Especially lately." She already missed him. "Brian is supposed to leave next week. But I'm determined to rest in the knowledge that nothing is impossible for God."

"That's right. It'll be cool to see how the Lord works everything out."

"Sure will." Talia set down her glass and sent up a quick prayer.

❧

Brian set aside the book he'd just finished reading on nutritional healing. He couldn't find medical fault with the author's argument, and he clearly understood how a combination of diet plus natural and homeopathic therapies could better a person's health. Perhaps those were the two elements missing from his own practice.

Standing, he walked into the kitchen area where he pulled a bottle of filtered water from the refrigerator. Opening the cap, he took a long swig. After ambling back into the open-concept living room of the cabin, he plopped down on the sofa. He thought about what Talia had said weeks ago. "God calls us to a balance."

Brian believed it.

He also knew without a doubt that he loved Talia Fountain. She was good for him, countering his introspective moods with her outgoing, fun personality. But his feelings for her complicated matters in the way he'd feared from the start. Now, in addition to one decision, Brian was forced to make two.

And next week was Labor Day. He was supposed to return to the clinic on Tuesday. Would the clinic's administrator consider adding a health food store to the ever-growing facility? Knowing the guy, if it made money, he'd be all for the idea.

But would Talia? She seemed bent on defending that historic building she loved so much. Did she love it more than him? Did she even love him at all?

What was a smitten guy like him to do?

Standing, Brian stretched before making his way out onto porch. Soon, the divine reply came loud and clear.

Minutes later, he headed for the pier. When the going gets tough, the tough go fishing.

Walking to the edge of the dock, the echo of a car door slamming at the top of the bluff reached his ears. He turned to face the sound, wondering who'd come to visit.

"Brian?"

Recognizing the voice, he smiled. "Down here, Talia. By the lake."

Soon, she was on her way down the dirt pathway. Her ankle was healing nicely, although she still walked with a slight limp.

He jogged over to meet her. "Be careful, I don't want you to reinjure—"

At that moment, she stumbled over a tree root. Brian ran to break her fall. He caught her around the waist just in time.

"I don't want you reinjuring yourself." He grinned into her startled face.

"I'm such a klutz."

"But you're a very pretty klutz."

Talia shook her head and pushed several light brown tendrils off her forehead. "Have you had your eyes checked lately?"

He chuckled, but he wished she wouldn't be so self-depreciating. In his opinion, Talia Fountain was a beautiful person—inside and out. He'd come to admire the many facets of her character as well as her personal convictions. Now, he wanted to marry her before some other guy noticed what a rare gem Talia Fountain really was.

"You wouldn't believe what happened today," she said. "I couldn't wait to tell you, so I rushed over here."

"What is it?" He still held her, although Talia found her footing.

"I suppose in one sense, it could be considered bad news, but I don't think so."

Brian gave her his undivided attention.

"Dirk Butterfield strutted into my store this afternoon and announced he'd purchased the building that *Fountain of Life* is located in. He said there was no longer a need for a town hall meeting, and now that he owned the property, he planned to develop it."

"I thought Blossom Lake owned the building."

"Butterfield has friends in high places." Her brow furrowed momentarily. "But, you know what? I don't care. While Butterfield restated his plans to demolish that wonderful relic, I kept thinking of what the Bible says in Second Peter, about the day of the Lord coming like a thief in the night..."

"...in which the heavens will pass away with a great noise, and the elements will melt with fervent heat; both the earth and the works that are in it will be burned up."

Talia gave a nod. "You see? It doesn't matter. Buildings will come and go, but my faith, my beliefs, are cemented in a firm foundation that lies deep within my soul. Because of Jesus Christ, neither Dirk Butterfield nor anyone else can destroy them."

Brian stroked her soft cheek with the backs of his fingers. "You're a wise woman, Tal."

A mischievous gleam entered her sparkling brown eyes. "I took my Ginkgo Biloba today. It's ideal for mental alertness."

"Oh, is that it?" Brian chuckled. She made him laugh, she touched his heart, she occupied his thoughts—what more could a man want? "Will you marry me?" He pulled her close.

"Whoa! Where did that come from?"

"My heart."

The surprise on Talia's face vanished. Tenderness shone in her eyes. "Oh, Brian—"

"Hey, Tal, what's going on down there?"

Her eyes widened. "Did I forget to mention that my father drove me here and that he was waiting for me in the car?"

"Um, yeah, I think you might have forgotten that little detail."

"Oops."

"How long does it take to tell the doc one simple thing?" Frank bellowed, his deep voice carrying across the lake like a foghorn.

"Hang on, Dad," Talia shouted back. "Brian's proposing to me." She returned her gaze to his. "Sorry 'bout that. Now where were we?"

"I believe I already proposed. I'm waiting for your reply."

"Are you sure you know what you're getting into?"

"That wasn't the question. The question was, will *you* marry *me*?"

"But I haven't met your family yet."

"You will," he promised, wondering at her hesitation. "And they'll love you because I do."

"Oh, Brian..." Her bright smile nearly stretched from one silver loop earring to the other. "Those are the words I've longed to hear." She looked as though she might melt in his arms. "I'm in love with you too, and, yes, I'll marry you. You're the first man to ever sweep me off my feet...literally."

"So how long does it take to say 'yes?'" Frank hollered down the hill. "For pity sakes, it's dinnertime!"

Talia groaned and sent a glance heavenward.

Brian chuckled. "C'mon, let's not keep your dad waiting."

He assisted Talia up the winding pathway until they met Frank in all his impatience, standing by the car.

"Well?" He spread his arms out. "What's the verdict?"

Talia grinned. "I'm going to marry him."

"Thank God." Frank smiled his approval, and Brian breathed a little easier.

Frank clasped his hand in a hearty congratulatory shake. "What about your medical practice, Doc?"

"It's still there. And it can stay there—without me. I have something else in mind."

Talia faced him. "Like what?"

"Like a clinic that promotes the art of nutritional healing as well as medical science." He arched a brow. "Will you partner with me?"

"I would be honored." She clasped her hands, looking positively giddy. "It's an incredible idea. I wish I thought of it."

Brian grinned, a little giddy himself.

"You thinkin' of openin' this practice in Blossom Lake, Doc?"

Brian nodded. "I love it up here."

"Okay, so when's the weddin'?" Frank rubbed his palms together.

"Soon." Brian fixed his eyes on Talia. "I don't want a long engagement."

"Me neither." She tipped her head. "What about a Christmas wedding?" A faraway look entered her brown eyes. "I can picture it now, the gold trim and white lights, my bridesmaids wearing burgundy-colored dresses."

"A Christmas wedding it is." Brian glanced at his father-in-law to be. "Any objections, Frank?"

"None. I'm rejoicing that I can finally marry her off."

Talia's expression went from winsome to annoyance. "Oh, Dad!"

Grinning, Brian opened the car door for her.

"You'd better come along, Doc," Frank said, starting the engine. "Marlene will want to discuss wedding plans."

Talia turned to him and reached for his hand. "Yes, Brian, please come over for dinner tonight."

"I'd enjoy it. Thanks." A grin worked at the corners of his mouth before he kissed the backs of her fingers. "And to think, our love began with your mother's marvelous apple pies..."

# Marlene's Marvelous Apple Pie

PAT-IN-PAN CRUST

1 ½ cup unbleached flour

2 t sugar

1 t salt

½ cup oil

2 T whole milk

Combine first 3 ingredients. Add oil and milk. Blend well, and pat into a 9-inch pie pan. Flute edges. Fill with apple filling (see below).

APPLE FILLING

6 cups peeled and sliced apples

½ cup sugar

3 T tapioca

½ t cinnamon

¼ t nutmeg

¼ t salt

½ t fresh lemon juice

Mix all ingredients but the apples. Once blended, add apple slices to mixture. Pour into pie shell and top with streusel (see below).

STREUSEL TOPPING

½ cup unbleached flour

¼ cup oatmeal

½ cup packed brown sugar

½ t cinnamon

½ cup butter

Combine all ingredients until mixture is crumbly. Sprinkle over fruit filling.

Bake pie at 425° for 40-45 minutes or until bubbly. Cover pie with tin foil for the last 10 minutes if the top starts getting too brown.

September Sonata

# Dedication

To my son, Pastor Ben Boeshaar, a volunteer fireman and chaplain for the sheriff's department, and a spiritual "fireman," leading people to Christ. May God richly bless you for your service.

# Prologue

*June*
*Milwaukee, Wisconsin*

ICY FEAR GRIPPED Kristin Robinson's heart as she raced down the emergency room's stark corridor.

A dark-haired woman in blue scrubs stepped into her path. "Can I help you?"

"I...I'm looking for my husband," Krissy panted, halting in mid-stride. "His name is Blaine Robinson. He's a fireman, and he was injured—"

"Yes, I know who you mean. Follow me."

The nurse led her into a bustling area where doctors, nurses, and secretaries conducted business matters around an island containing desks and computers. Reaching the last room in a row of six, the woman opened a sliding glass door. There, right before Krissy's eyes, lay her husband, stretched out on a hospital gurney. His face was blackened with soot, and his hair and skin smelled singed by the hungry flames that had obviously sought to devour him.

"Blaine," she choked, rushing to his bedside. She noticed the blue and white hospital gown he wore, and the lightweight blanket covering him from the waist down. "Are you all right? I came as soon as I could."

"I'm okay, honey." He peeked at her through one open eye. "I fell through the roof and injured my back. Looks like I cracked a couple of vertebrae."

"Oh, Blaine, no!"

"Now, don't worry. It's not as bad as it sounds. Could have been worse. I'm praising the Lord that my spinal cord is intact. I can move my feet, wiggle my toes...sure hurts, though." He winced as if to prove his point.

"Blaine..."

With tears pricking the backs of her eyes, Krissy lifted his hand and held it between both of hers. In all their twenty years of marriage, this is what she'd feared the most—an injury in the line of duty. How many endless nights had she lain awake worrying that he'd never come home again to her and their two daughters? She was also well aware that firefighters faced the possibility of death each and every time they responded to a call. By now, one would think that Krissy was accustomed to the ever-present threat. Today, however, when she'd received the phone call informing her that Blaine had been hurt, it was like reliving the nightmare.

"Hon, I'm going to make a full recovery," Blaine assured her, his eyelids heavy with whatever the nurses gave him for pain. "The emergency room doc said the orthopedic surgeon on call is coming to speak with us. I'll probably undergo surgery to help my back heal, and after a few months of recuperation, I'll be as good as new." He paused, grinning beneath the filmy soot covering his mouth. "Maybe even better..."

*One*

*Eight Weeks Later...*

"ARE YOU SURE you're up to driving?" Krissy asked Blaine as they headed north in their minivan. They'd dropped their twin daughters off at a Christian college in Florida and traveled most of the day. According to Krissy's calculations, they had another seventeen hours to go before they reached Wisconsin. Since Blaine was still recovering from his back surgery, she didn't want him to overdo it. "Would you like me to take the wheel for a while?"

"I'm fine," he replied, "but I think we'll stop at a motel in Knoxville."

Krissy's nod belied her sense of misgiving. Her husband wasn't all that "fine" if he intended to stop for the night. Not Mr. Drive-till-we-get-there Blaine Robinson. His back was most likely aching from all the activity this week. He'd loaded and unloaded the girls' belongings in and out of the van, and carried items into their dormitory that he probably shouldn't have lifted.

Krissy glanced over at the profile that, in the past two decades, had become as familiar as her own face. Blaine's chestnut-brown hair was tinged with just a hint of grey above the ears, and in the last five years, a bald spot had appeared at the crown of his head that the girls liked to kiss just to irritate him. His skin was tanned from the summer sunshine since he took advantage of convalescing outdoors. His neck and shoulders were thick with muscles he'd developed lifting heavy fire hoses and other equipment while he'd been on the job, although his mid-section was getting awfully wide these days. Krissy didn't want to mention it, but she figured he'd put on about twenty pounds in the last three months. Worse, he'd gotten lazy and slack when it came to his appearance. All these years, they'd both tried to take care of themselves and keep fit, but lately, Blaine had let himself go. It was rather disappointing.

Still, she loved him. He was the man with whom she would spend the remainder of her life...but why did that suddenly sound like such a long time?

"It's kind of weird without Mandy and Laina around," Krissy stated on a rueful note.

"Yeah, I think the girls chattered the entire way to Florida."

Krissy grinned. "They did...and now it's too quiet in here."

Blaine apparently decided to remedy the matter by turning the radio on to the Rush Limbaugh show.

"Must you really subject me to this?" Krissy complained. "You listen to this guy every day."

"Yeah, so?" Blaine took his eyes off the road for a moment and looked over at her through his fashionable sunglasses.

"I don't care for some of his views," Krissy said.

"Well, I do, and with the presidential election coming up in November, I want to stay informed."

Krissy gritted her teeth and leaned back in the seat, closing her eyes and trying not to hear the male voice booming conservative credos through the stereo speakers. While she considered herself a conservative Christian, she simply found the popular radio talk show host, in a word, annoying. In the last eight weeks, while Blaine recuperated, Krissy tolerated his penchant for the program. But now, as a captive audience, she resented being...trapped.

She opened her eyes and leaned forward abruptly. "Blaine, can't we compromise? Surely there's another news station we could listen to."

"Relax. This show is only on for another hour and then I'll change the channel if you want."

Won't be any reason to change the channel then, she silently fumed.

Krissy turned her head toward the window and watched the scenery go by. It was only late August, but already some treetops were turning gold, orange and russet. Autumn had begun in the Smoky and Appalachian mountains. And next week, Krissy would be back at school, teaching third graders. She mulled over everything she needed to do in preparation. This year would be much different than the past twelve since Grace Christian School, the elementary school in which she'd taught, had merged with a larger institution due to financial constraints. Krissy expected changes, but she tried not to worry about them. Monday would come soon enough.

The minutes ticked by, and finally, the ragging on the liberals ceased. Blaine pressed the radio buttons until he found classical music. Krissy's taut nerves began to relax.

"Better?" Blaine asked, a slight smirk curving his well-shaped mouth.

"Much. Thanks." Krissy couldn't seem to help the note of cynicism in her reply. Then she paused, listening. "I don't recognize this piece."

Blaine gave it a moment's deliberation. "I believe it's one of Mozart's sonatas, obviously for the violin and piano."

"Obviously." Krissy quipped, smiling. Over the years, she acquired a taste for the classics, although she hadn't ever learned to discern the various artists' styles, let alone the titles. "And tell me again how a sonata differs from, say, a waltz or serenade."

"A waltz is basically dance music written in triple time with the accent on the first beat."

"Ah, yes, that's right."

"A sonata is written in three or four movements."

"It's coming back to me now," Krissy said.

Blaine chuckled. "After enjoying this music for twenty years, you should be an expert."

"Yes, I suppose I should."

"Well, after another twenty," Blaine stated in jest, "you're bound to be a fine critic of classic music."

An odd, sinking feeling enveloped Krissy. Symphonies and overtures were Blaine's forte, not hers. He was an accomplished musician himself and played the piano, although he hadn't practiced in years. Regardless, she'd developed knowledge and respect for the art because of him and had to admit that Brahms, Beethoven, and Mozart did have a way with soothing her jangled nerves after a long day at school. Nevertheless, she enjoyed other types of music as much or more. In fact, she and their daughters liked to attend musicals, both in Chicago and Milwaukee. They had seen "Show Boat" and "Phantom of the Opera" and...

*But the girls are adults and in college now, Krissy thought. Blaine and I have the rest of our lives...together. Alone.*

The reality of her situation suddenly struck with full force. There were no more children to care for, fret over, shop with, cook for. No more parent-teacher conferences, basketball and football games to watch as her lovely daughters cheered on their high school's team. Although Amanda and Alaina were twins, they weren't identical, and each possessed her own fun personality that Krissy now realized she would sorely miss. Tears began to well in her eyes and spill down her cheeks. She sniffed and reached for her purse to find a tissue.

"What's the matter?"

"Oh, nothing."

"What?" Blaine pursued. "It's not the radio show, is it? It's over now."

"No, no...it's the girls. They're gone." Krissy's tears flowed all the harder now. Her babies. Grown up. Living far away from home. Why, she'd become so preoccupied with helping them prepare and pack for college, not to mention nursing Blaine back to health, that she hadn't realized the impact their daughters' departure would have. "They grew up so fast," Krissy said, blowing hard into the tissue. "Where did the years go?"

"Oh, for pity sake..." Blaine's exasperation sounded loud and clear. But then he reached across the built-in plastic console in the center of the two front seats and stroked the back of her hair. "Sweetheart, the girls'll be back." His voice softened. "In a few months, it's Christmas. A short while after that, they'll be home for summer vacation...and you'll never get a moment's peace because of all the yakking they do."

Krissy managed a smile. "You're right," she said with a little sniffle. "I'm being silly." She thought it over and breathed a sigh. "I only wish we would have had more children."

"That's a ridiculous wish, and you know it." Blaine removed his hand and placed both palms on the steering wheel. "We tried, but God didn't see fit to give us any more kids. Instead, Mandy and Laina were a double blessing. Still are. Always will be."

Krissy couldn't argue. Their twin daughters were a special gift from God.

"Think of it this way," Blaine continued, a smile in his deep voice, "we're still young. You and I have the rest of our lives together."

Krissy winced, and fresh tears filled her eyes. How could she tell Blaine that the very words he spoke to cheer her up depressed her? She wasn't exactly feeling like the godly, submissive wife of which the Bible speaks, yet her emotions were real, and she didn't know how to handle them. True, she and Blaine had "the rest of their lives," but what would they do with all those years together? She loved him, but somehow the deep sentiment didn't seem enough. In the past twenty years, Blaine was gone more than he'd been home, and Krissy had been a busy mother and school teacher. Of course, she and Blaine would continue to progress in their careers, but was that all their lives together amounted to? Separate occupations? Separate lives, joined together by a vow to have and to hold, for better or for worse...till death do us part?

&#x2766;

"What's eating you?" Blaine asked later as he lay on one of the double beds in the motel room wearing nothing but his white T-shirt and navy-printed boxers. Beneath his knees, Krissy placed three pillows to ease his back discomfort. Unfortunately, she couldn't do anything about the atmosphere. Increasing her melancholy was the fact that the air conditioning unit didn't work well, and the room felt hot and stuffy on this sweltering August night in Knoxville, Tennessee. "You haven't said more than five words since we stopped for supper."

"Oh, I'm just tired." Krissy decided that had to be it. Exhaustion. Sitting in a nearby floral-upholstered armchair, she stared blindly at the newscast on television. Maybe once she got back home and fell into a routine, teaching during the day, correcting homework in the evenings, she wouldn't miss the girls so much.

"Go take a cold shower," Blaine suggested. "It did wonders for me."

"Good idea."

She gazed at him again, noticing for the first time that his brawny frame took up most of the bed. They slept on a king-size mattress at home. Last night, they'd rented a motel room with the same size bed. But tonight, this room with two doubles was all the desk clerk could offer them if they preferred a nonsmoking environment—which they did. If Blaine weren't healing from back surgery, Krissy wouldn't hesitate to tell him to move over, but it appeared she was destined to sleep alone.

Separate lives. Separate beds. What a way to start the rest of their lives together.

# *Two*

BLAINE WATCHED KRISSY back the minivan out of the driveway before shifting gears and accelerating down the street. He couldn't figure out the change in her. She'd been glum for the past few days. He'd first concluded she missed the girls. But after overhearing her talking to them on a conference call on her cell phone yesterday afternoon, he thought Krissy had snapped out of it. She encouraged the girls like a regular cheerleader. Now, however, Blaine wondered if there was more to Krissy's doldrums.

So he questioned her.

In reply, she had merely shrugged and admitted she didn't have a clue as to what was wrong.

Blaine moved away from the living room windows. After today, Krissy would be teaching school again. Maybe getting back to work would cheer her up, except Blaine wished it was him returning to his job.

Walking into the kitchen, he grinned at the red apples on green vines that Krissy and the girls had papered onto the walls not even a month ago. They'd urged him to stay out of their way while they wet and hung pieces of wallpaper. They giggled and chattered all the while, and Blaine had no problem finding something else to do.

Females. After living with three of them for twenty years, Blaine still couldn't figure them out half the time.

He continued grinning as he poured himself a cup of coffee. Taking a sip, he thought over Krissy's odd mood swings, then recalled what she'd said about her new school, its principal, and the other teachers. He figured she was most likely suffering from a case of nerves. And, come to think of it, it was that time of month. He heaved a sigh. Well, whatever bothered her, she'd snap out of it.

Blaine glanced at the clock and realized he needed to hurry and shower in order to make it to his physical therapy appointment. Pushing thoughts of Krissy from his mind, he set down the ceramic mug and headed for the bathroom.

⤳

Krissy gazed around at all the enthusiastic faces in the conference room of Wellsprings Academy. She was one of the older teachers here. Surrounding her were five other women, all appearing to have just graduated from college, and three men who couldn't be any older than the Academy's principal, Matt Sawyer, who was about thirty-something. As Mr. Sawyer detailed his plans for the upcoming year, Krissy wondered if she really belonged at this place.

"I'd like every teacher to get personally involved with his or her students' education this year," the principal said, and when his gaze came her way, Krissy noticed how blue his eyes were, how strong his jaw line seemed, how tall he stood, and how broad his shoulders looked beneath the crisp, white dress shirt he wore.

Was he married? A moment later, she berated herself for even allowing the question to take form in her mind. *I'm married, and I love my husband!* A nauseating fist cinched her gut. How could she find another man attractive?

What was wrong with her? Nothing seemed right since Blaine's accident and the girls beginning college. When no divine reply was forthcoming, Krissy gave herself a mental shake and forced her thoughts back to the meeting.

At the mid-morning break, Krissy helped herself to a cup of steaming coffee that had been set up on a long, narrow table in the hallway. She deliberated over all the delectable treats, also on display, and chose a small cinnamon muffin.

"Those are my favorite."

Krissy turned to find Matt Sawyer standing directly behind her. Krissy froze as he reached around her and plucked a muffin from the plastic plate.

"Well, what do you think so far?" he asked.

She pushed out a polite smile. "I think your staff is very young."

He grinned and took a bite of his muffin. As he chewed, his blue eyes wandered around, taking in the other mingling teachers. "They're all qualified educators, believe me."

"Oh, I'm sure they are. It's just that...well, I don't see any of the teachers I worked with last year."

"They seemed competent and experienced. I read each one's resume. Unfortunately, we only needed one third grade teacher since Leslie Comings got married this past summer."

Krissy couldn't believe her ears. "You mean to tell me I'm the only teacher who didn't lose her job?"

"Combining two schools isn't as simple as it might seem, I'm afraid. There were no easy decisions for the board members. The truth of the matter is the merger didn't warrant extra teachers— even with the addition of Grace Christian School's populace."

"I see." Her heart ached for her former colleagues.

"But we're glad you're here...Kristin, isn't it?"

She nodded.

"I've always been partial to the name. If I had a daughter, I would have liked to name her Kristin."

She smiled nervously, unsure of how to respond. "Well, thank you, Mr. Sawyer."

He grinned. "Call me Matt. We're all in this together, and I think we should be on a first name basis, don't you?"

"Sure." She'd been on a first name basis with the principal of Grace Christian School. The solidly built, gray-headed man had been a father-figure to her when situations arose in the classroom and Krissy wanted advice. But somehow, she couldn't imagine herself running to Matt Sawyer's office for morsels of wisdom and seasoned counsel. The guy was too charming. Too...threatening.

"So you, um, have no daughters?" Krissy figured that bringing up his family life would deter her attraction to him. "You and your wife have sons?"

"I have neither a wife nor children." A rueful-looking expression crossed his handsome features. "My wife is dead. She committed suicide about three years ago."

Krissy sucked in a horrified gasp.

"It's no secret around here," Matt continued, "and I find being open about the tragedy has helped me recover."

"I'm sure, but still...I'm so sorry to hear of your loss."

"Thank you." He paused and took another bite of his muffin. "My wife struggled with severe depression, but it comforts me to know she was a believer." He finished the rest of his baked treat. "I've often wondered, though, what Julie said to the Lord when she met Him. I imagine He put His loving arms around her and...and wiped away all tears from her eyes. He probably assured her that there would be no more death, neither sorrow, nor crying, and no more pain."

Krissy recognized the paraphrase from the Book of Revelation, saw the faraway, mournful look in Matt's gaze, and marveled at the depth of his sensitivity. She could well envision their loving Heavenly Father wrapping His loving arms around a hurting soul, one of His own, and wiping away her tears.

"Well, I hope you'll enjoy your year at Wellsprings Academy." Matt snapped from his reverie.

Krissy blinked. "Thanks." She smiled, more naturally this time.

"And I'll look forward to getting to know you better," he added with a light in his blue eyes.

"Same here." The words were out of her mouth before Krissy even realized she'd spoken them.

❧

Blaine groaned in pain as he lowered himself onto the padded lawn chair in the back yard. His physical therapy session took a toll on him today. He'd used muscles in his back he hadn't realized he possessed. Unfortunately, instead of feeling better, he felt more disabled than ever. Glancing around the yard, he longed to pull out the weed-whacker and get rid of the some of the growth inching upward through the patio blocks. He wished he could mow the lawn. This summer, Krissy and the girls took turns and, while they did an adequate job, they didn't mow it the way Blaine preferred, but he didn't complain. How could he? He'd been little more than vegetation, supervising from the lawn chair.

"Hi, Blaine." The cool feminine voice wafted over the wooden fence from the yard next door. "It's certainly hot this afternoon."

Lifting an eyelid, he glimpsed his neighbor, Jill, wearing nothing but a little halter-top and a skimpy pair of shorts. He closed his eyes again. "Hi yourself. Pardon me for not being a gentleman and getting up. The truth is, my back hurts and I can't move."

Jill's soft laugh wafted to his ears. "Give me a break. Even flat on your back you're a gentleman."

Stretched out in the shady part of the yard, Blaine grinned at the remark. It felt good to be complimented.

"I wish Ryan was as much a gentleman as you."

Hearing the anguish in her voice, Blaine's heart filled with sympathy. His neighbors weren't exactly the happily married couple that he and Krissy were. During the summer months, with the windows open, sounds of their feuding drifted over the property line nearly every night. Blaine and Krissy had shared the Good News with the pair, inviting them out to attend a Bible study and church, but Ryan and Jill stated vehemently that they weren't "into religion." Regardless, prayers continued on their behalf.

"Did the girls get off to college all right?" Jill wanted to know.

"Yep. They called this weekend and seem to be doing fine. They like their roommates."

"Think they'll get homesick?"

"Probably."

Jill laughed and Blaine prayed she'd quit her chatting and tend to the toddler yelping inside her house. Nothing grated on his nerves more than a bawling child. Krissy said the neighbors' bickering bothered her more than their kids' temper tantrums. Blaine, on the other hand, had no problem tuning out the arguing, but the kids' fussing made him edgy.

"I'll sure miss Mandy and Laina," Jill said. "They were such handy babysitters."

"They'll be back."

"Yeah, but my sanity might be gone by then." The child's wailing increased. "Well, I'd better go. See ya later."

"Sure, Jill. See ya."

Blaine opened his eyes in time to see his neighbor stoop near the sandbox and retrieve two small navy-blue sneakers. She shook the sand off them then entered the house.

Left alone to relax once more, Blaine thanked God that those days of sandboxes, diapers, and crying children were behind him. He recalled how he'd enjoyed leaving the house for work just because he knew he wouldn't be back for thirty-six hours. Thirty-six hours without listening to kids cry. Krissy, of course, handled things much better than he did. She never complained. Not once. She never seemed to get upset or impatient with the twins. They turned out to be sweet young ladies, largely because of her, although Blaine had made it a point to be part of their lives as much as possible. He'd enjoyed his daughters from the time they were about six years old. He coached their girls' softball team in the summertime and gymnastics team during the winter months. He involved himself with the youth group at church and chaperoned outings and events whenever his schedule permitted, and he held fond memories of his daughters' growing up years. But he was glad they were over.

Off in the direction of the garage, a car door slammed shut and Blaine realized Krissy had arrived home from work. He heard her enter the house and wondered how long it would take before she found him languishing here in the yard. She'd have to help him out of the lawn chair. He hadn't been lying to Jill when he said he couldn't move. Minutes later, much to his relief, Krissy appeared.

"Must be nice to lounge around all day," she quipped, her hands on her slender hips. The tepid autumn breeze tousled her blonde hair, causing it to brush lightly against the tops of her shoulders.

"Hey, you're a sight for sore eyes. Can you help me out of this chair?"

Krissy wagged her head, obviously over his pathetic state, and walked toward him. When she reached the edge of the lawn chair, she held out her hand. Blaine took it, but instead of allowing her to pull him up, he tugged, causing her to fall against him. Then he kissed her soundly, albeit awkwardly.

"Very funny." She worked herself into a sitting position on the side of the chair near Blaine's knees. "The two of us are liable to break this flimsy thing, and then you'll really have back problems."

Blaine sighed. "I suppose you're right."

"As always." Krissy discreetly tucked her denim dress beneath her.

"How was your day?" he asked.

"Not too bad. And yours?"

"In a word...painful."

"Sorry to hear it." Krissy stood and helped Blaine to his feet. Lightening-hot pain bolted down his lower spine and thighs, blinding him for about ten seconds.

"Are you okay, Blaine?"

"Yeah." He forced a smile, not wanting to worry her. "What's for supper?"

"I don't know. What are you hungry for?"

"Not sure."

"We're a decisive team."

Blaine grinned and set his arm around Krissy's shoulders, leaning on her as they walked toward the house. He didn't inquire further about her day. Didn't need to. His wife seemed to be her old self again.

# *Three*

"MIND IF I use you for a pillow?"

Krissy bristled. "Do I look like a pillow?"

Blaine grinned. "You're soft and curvy. You'll do."

Unable to help a grin, Krissy scooted over and made room for Blaine on the couch. He stretched out, his head at the far end while he lifted his legs onto her lap.

"I need something under my knees when I lie down," he explained. "I think that's why I couldn't get myself out of the lawn chair earlier."

"I'm honored that you've selected me as your cushion." Krissy couldn't keep the sarcasm out of her voice. "Nice to know I'm good for something around here other than cooking, cleaning, and playing nurse and taxi-cab driver to a convalescing husband."

"Playing nurse is my favorite," Blaine shot back with a mischievous gleam in his eyes. "I only wish I could enjoy it more."

Shaking her head at him, Krissy lifted her feet onto the coffee table and set aside her now-empty paper plate. She and Blaine had finally decided to order out tonight. He wanted Italian and she wanted Chinese, and neither would compromise, so Krissy ended up making two stops.

"How was your supper?"

"Great," Blaine replied. "Yours?"

"Marvelous. Sweet and sour chicken is my ultimate favorite."

"The stuff gives me gas. Are you sure that Chinese place uses chicken? Hard to tell with all the breading and sauce."

"Oh, quiet. Of course it's chicken."

Blaine chuckled and Krissy rested her hands on his navy wind-pants. "One of the guys at work told me this joke about a Chinese Restaurant."

"I don't want to hear it."

"Something about a cat in the kettle at the Peking Room."

"Blaine, I said I don't want to hear your rotten joke!"

He laughed. She clamped her jaw and tamped down her mounting irritation. Why did he always have to poke fun at her food? She would never do such a thing to him...not that he'd let an unsavory joke spoil his appetite.

She tried to squelch her exasperation by allowing her gaze to wander around their lower-level family room. The walls were paneled with knotty pine and decorated with various family snapshots that ranged from Blaine and Krissy's wedding to the twins' first steps to their graduating from high school last May. As she recalled each special event, a wave of nostalgia crashed over her.

Her annoyed feelings forgotten for the moment, she turned to Blaine. She'd intended to engage him in a match of "remember when," but noticed that he'd begun to doze. Disappointed, Krissy stared at the television. Watching the handsome, syndicated talk show host, she noticed the similarity between his strong jaw line and Matt Sawyer's. A little smile tugged at the corners of her mouth.

Yes, the principal of Wellsprings Academy could certainly dub for a celebrity with his good looks and charming manner. Krissy couldn't help but wonder why he didn't remarry. She imagined Matt would most likely say it was because he hadn't "found the right one." That seemed to be a standard line among single people these days. However, Krissy noticed that there were a number of unattached, pretty females teaching at the Academy, and she guessed it wouldn't be long before the "right one" walked into Matt's life.

Within moments, her musings took flight and she speculated on the sort of woman it would take to win Matt's heart. Obviously, he'd been devastated when his first wife committed suicide, so the next woman to enter his life would have to somehow dispel all the doubts and fears born from such a tragedy. Krissy knew what she'd do if she weren't married. She'd cultivate a friendship with the man, learning all his likes and dislikes, and she would be quick to point out the interests they shared. Like reading, for instance. This afternoon, while Krissy acquainted herself with her new classroom, Matt had stopped by with a novel in his hands.

"Have you by any chance read this book?"

Spying the cover, Krissy recognized it, nodded, and rambled off an impromptu quote that she recalled from the story.

"Yes, that's the one." Matt grinned. "I'm enjoying it very much."

"I recall it was a very touching story."

"Quite. And the *Left Behind* series...have you read it?"

"Every book."

"What's your take on the novels?"

For nearly an hour, they discussed books and shared their perspectives on various authors, styles, and storylines. Krissy found the conversation refreshing, since she'd been trying for two decades to get Blaine interested in reading. But he only enjoyed it if the topics pertained to sports or firefighting, and he couldn't appreciate anything longer than a newspaper's feature article.

She glanced over at Blaine now, expecting to find him snoozing. But to her outright chagrin, she discovered him staring back at her.

"What are you thinking about?" he asked softly. His eyes seemed to scrutinize her every feature.

Krissy felt her cheeks redden with embarrassment. "Books. I was thinking about books."

"Mm..."

Blaine's gaze was like a weighty probe, searching the innermost parts of her being. At that moment, Krissy felt like the wickedest woman ever to roam Wisconsin. Here she ought to be enjoying her husband's company, but instead, she was dreaming of capturing another man's heart.

*Forgive me, Lord, she silently prayed. What's wrong with me?*

Krissy crawled out from under Blaine's knees then placed a large throw pillow beneath them.

"I'm tired. I think I'll turn in."

"Sure. Good night, hon."

"'Night."

Heavy-hearted and feeling more than just a tad guilty, Krissy made her way upstairs to the master bedroom.

❧

That was weird. Blaine watched Krissy's departure. He'd never seen such an odd expression on her face. She'd been daydreaming, that was obvious. But about books? No way. If she had said she'd been thinking about the girls and remembering some silly thing the three of them did together, Blaine would have bought it, lock, stock, and barrel. Unfortunately, he didn't buy it at all, and a slight foreboding sent a chill up his already aching spine. What was with Krissy these days?

Time to find out.

With a determined set to his jaw, he roused himself from the couch and made his way upstairs. He walked down the hallway of their ranch home, heading for their room. When he reached the doorway, however, he stopped short, seeing Krissy on her knees at the side of the bed, her Bible open on the floral spread in front of her. Silently, Blaine stepped backwards, retracing his steps to the living room where he decided to put off any discussion until she finished her time with the Lord.

Nearly twenty minutes later, he heard the bathroom door close, followed by sounds of the shower spray.

Great. She could be in there all night.

Well, fine, he'd wait for Krissy in the bedroom. Once more, he ambled down the hallway and entered their room. Lowering himself onto the bed, Blaine tucked a pillow beneath his knees, turned on the small television, and began his vigil.

⌒♈⌒

Krissy heard him before she ever saw him. Blaine. Snoring loudly. On top of their bed. And with her pillow under his knees, no less. Had he worn those wind-pants all day? To physical therapy with a lot of sick people around? Wonderful. Like she really wanted to place her head on it now!

Irritation coursed through her veins as she slipped into her nightie. Did Blaine ever once think of her? Couldn't he respect her

115

feelings on anything, be it carryout food or books or her own, personal pillow?

With a huff, she grabbed the remote from where it lay on Blaine's rounded, t-shirt encased belly, and turned off the TV. Next, she switched off the lamp and stomped out of the room, intending to sleep in one of the girls' beds tonight. She longed to slam the door but refrained from doing so. Still, she wasn't quiet about putting clean sheets on Mandy's bed.

Even so, Blaine never awoke.

# *Four*

BLAINE YAWNED AND stumbled into the kitchen. "How come you slept in Mandy's room last night?"

Krissy threw him an annoyed glance then whirled around and finished preparing a pot of coffee. Already dressed for school, she looked quite attractive in the blue and green plaid cotton skirt and hunter-green T-shirt. The outfit complimented her blonde hair and tanned skin.

"All right, Krissy, spit it out. What's up with you these days?"

She flipped on the automatic brewing device and it made its usual chugging. Turning to face him again, she folded her arms.

"Well?" Blaine demanded.

"Nothing is 'up with me.'"

"Nothing? It's hardly nothing, Kris." He eased himself into a chair at the kitchen table. "You've been acting so strange, ever since the girls went off to school. I mean..." He searched his mind for the right words. "Sometimes I feel like I don't even know you anymore. Like last night. I've got the sense you weren't daydreaming about books. So what was going through your head?"

He watched as she blushed slightly before lifting her chin. She appeared almost defiant—another trait unlike the Krissy he'd married.

"I think you said it all," she answered softly, "when you said you don't know me anymore. In all honesty, you don't."

"What in the world are you talking about?"

"It's true." She avoided his gaze, her voice wavering. "We never talk like we used to, and when I try to discuss a topic of importance to me, you never listen. You don't even know what's going on in my life these days. You think you do, but really you don't."

He took a sip from the steaming mug she set in front of him and tried to think how he should handle this. Maybe it was just hormones. Sometimes, when she got this way, it was simply a matter of riding out the storm.

As if she'd read his mind, she spat, "And don't think this is a premenstrual syndrome thing. It's not. This is something I've been aware of for a long time now. An intricate part of our marriage is gone, and it's never been more prevalent since your accident. You and I, Blaine, have nothing in common. We're two people who are married and live under one roof, but we're not one flesh. Not anymore."

Blaine narrowed his gaze, feeling more than a little disturbed by what he'd just heard. "Krissy, are you...are you thinking...?"

He couldn't get himself to say the word "divorce." The mere idea caused his gut to knot up.

"Krissy," he began again, "you and I made vows to each other—"

"I'm not about to break my wedding vows," she shot back.

"Okay. Good."

"We're stuck with each other...for the rest of our lives."

Blaine's jaw slacked. "Did you just say 'stuck with each other?'"

Krissy had the good grace to look chagrined.

"Stuck? Is that how you see it?"

"I'm going to be late." She marched quickly past him and grabbed her bag lunch and purse.

Blaine rose from the chair. "Wait."

She didn't. "See you tonight. As usual."

She exited the side door before he could stop her. Disbelief enveloped him. Blaine listened to the van door slam, the engine roar to life, and the sounds of Krissy backing the vehicle out of the garage and down the driveway.

"Stuck with each other," Blaine whispered incredulously. Next came the tidal wave of hurt that threatened to submerge him in a mixture of sorrow and rage. He didn't feel "stuck" with her. He loved Krissy—loved her with all his heart. He'd do anything for her. But she felt "stuck" with him.

*First the rage. How can she be so selfish, thinking only of herself and what she wants? And what does she want anyhow? She's got everything. A house, a job she enjoys, a husband who loves her, two nearly perfect daughters...*

He fumed all the while he dressed. Then, as he drove to his doctor's appointment later in the morning, the agonizing sorrow gripped his heart. *She doesn't love me anymore. What does a guy do when his wife doesn't love him anymore? When did it happen? How come I never noticed?*

Blaine had heard of marriages crumbling once the kids were grown and gone. He would believe it'd happen to his next-door neighbors, but not to him and Krissy. They were Christians. This stuff wasn't supposed to happen to godly couples.

Perplexed, he drove into the clinic's parking structure, found a spot and pulled his truck to a halt.

"So how's the back?" Dr. Lemke asked about thirty minutes later. The man's bald head shone like a brand new plastic toy under the fluorescent lights in the exam room. Blaine would wager the short, stocky physician weighed about three hundred and fifty pounds, and he prayed he'd never end up fat and bald in his old age.

"Back's not so good. I'm still in a lot of pain."

The physician met his gaze. "Yes, so I see from the physical therapist's report. He states you're unable to do some pretty simple stretching and bending exercises."

"True, but don't think I haven't been practicing my exercises at home like the therapist told me. I'm doing them, but they're not helping."

"Hm..."

Blaine watched the pen tip wiggle as Dr. Lemke scratched down what they'd discussed. Since the man was employed by the City of Milwaukee, Blaine figured he wanted to write out a return-to-work slip as soon as possible and spare further workers' compensation. In truth, Blaine wanted that too. He was growing bored at home all day.

"I'm advising you to see a specialist," the doctor said at last. "Go back to the surgeon who operated. I'm afraid I can't do anything more for you."

"Sure. Whatever."

The doctor scribbled out the referral and his medical assistant made the appointment for Blaine. Sheet of paper in hand, he left the clinic and climbed painfully into his pick-up truck. He didn't care a whit about himself as he made the drive toward home. He kept thinking about what Krissy had said this morning.

*We're stuck with each other.*

She meant it, too. They'd said things to each before that they didn't mean, like most other married couples. They'd apologized for them, then prayed together and asked for God's forgiveness. But given Krissy's odd behavior of late, he could tell those words came from the very depth of her soul.

*Lord, what do I do?* He pulled into the driveway. Tears welled in his eyes, and he couldn't remember the last time he'd cried.

Again, he prayed, asking God to save his marriage. He'd be reduced to nothing without Krissy. She meant everything to him. *Lord, please help me. Please save my marriage. I'm nothing without Krissy.*

*Did you ever tell her that?*

The voice wasn't an audible one, but it served as the divine reply he sought.

Sure, I told her. Millions of times.

*Millions?*

And trillions.

Blaine shifted in the seat, uncomfortable as he suddenly couldn't recall when he'd last shared his heart with Krissy.

How many times does a guy have to tell his wife the same old thing?

*Millions and trillions.*

Blaine grinned and gazed up through his sunroof at the blue, cloudless sky. "All right, Lord. I get it. You don't have to hit me over the head with a brick."

Exiting his truck, he grimaced as a shooting pain blasted down his leg. "On second thought, maybe You did."

❧

"Mrs. Robinson, you have a phone call." Turning from the bulletin board she decorated, Krissy forced a smile at the secretary.

"I would have used the intercom system," the woman explained, "but it doesn't seem to be working. We'll have it fixed by the time school starts, though."

"Thanks. I'll be right there."

The tall, slim, redhead, whose age seemed unfathomable, nodded and exited the classroom. Krissy had heard Mrs. Sterling was pushing sixty, yet she looked and acted no older than thirty-five. Secretly, Krissy hoped she'd be in such good shape at that age.

Setting the stapler down on her desk, Krissy followed the woman up the hallway. They entered the office suite. Mrs. Sterling returned to her desk, and without even picking up the receiver, Krissy knew Blaine would be at the other end of the line. What had possessed her to throw such hateful words at him this morning? She was ashamed of herself all the way to school, and then Matt's morning "challenge" to all the teachers really touched her heart.

"Hello?" she answered somewhat timidly, wondering why he didn't call her cell phone. But then she recalled that she'd turned it off so she could concentrate on her work without interruptions.

"Hi, hon, what do you want for supper tonight?"

Blaine sounded like his same old self. Krissy relaxed. "Um, I really hadn't thought about it."

"Well, do you mind if I whip up something?"

She grimaced. Blaine was famous for his three-alarm chili at the fire station. Unfortunately, it wasn't one of Krissy's favorites. But she'd hurt him enough for one day. "Sure, make whatever you want."

"Okay."

"And, Blaine...?"

"Yeah?"

Krissy glanced over her shoulder to be sure no one could overhear. Mrs. Sterling was nowhere in sight. "Sorry about this morning..."

"Honey, all is forgiven, and we can talk about it tonight if you want."

"We can...talk?" Holding the phone several inches away, Krissy stared at it as if the piece of equipment had grown a mouth of its own. "All right," she said at last. "I'll see you in about an hour."

"Sounds good. And Kris...I love you."

She managed to smile despite the wave of guilt washing over her. She hung up the phone. Why was Blaine acting so nice after she'd been so mean? Of course, he wasn't a guy to stay angry or hold grudges, but he wasn't always so agreeable either.

"Everything all right, Kristin?" Pivoting, she watched Matt walk out of his private office and into the area in which the secretary sat. "You look like you got some bad news."

"No, no," she assured him. "I think the doctor gave my husband some different pain medication. He didn't sound like himself."

"Hm..." Matt gave her a curious frown. "Why does he take prescription drugs—if you don't mind me asking?"

"Oh, I don't mind." It was no secret, after all. "Blaine was injured at work. He's a fireman, and he fell through the roof of a two-story house. Cracked a couple of vertebrae and underwent surgery to repair a couple of discs that ruptured in the process."

"How horrible. When did that happen?"

"Last June."

"I see. Well, I'll pray for him. My deceased wife had back surgery, but it wasn't the success we hoped. In fact, her intense pain was a factor in her depression, which in turn brought about her addiction to prescription drugs."

Krissy sucked in a breath, hoping such a thing wouldn't befall Blaine. But she quickly shook off her misgivings. Blaine hadn't been depressed a day in his life. As for an addiction to pain medication, he rarely took the stuff—even when he legitimately needed it.

"I didn't mean to frighten you," Matt said, his expression earnest.

Krissy blinked. "No, no...you didn't scare me. You simply gave me something to think about."

"One thing I learned from the situation with my wife is that life is short. Too short to waste on unhappiness."

Krissy couldn't help agreeing. She'd felt dispirited for over a week, and it wasn't any fun.

Matt gave her a compassionate grin. "You can talk to me anytime. I'll be here for you."

A blush crept up Krissy's neck and warmed her cheeks. "That's very kind."

"I mean it."

"I know you do. Thanks."

Their gazes met and Krissy's traitorous heart began to hammer so loudly she was certain Matt could hear it. She was only too grateful when Mrs. Sterling re-entered the office, carrying a stack of papers.

Krissy quickly made her exit.

# *Five*

KRISSY TURNED THE van into the driveway and groaned at the sight of her next-door neighbor, Jill Nebhardt, standing near the patio wearing khaki shorts and red t-shirt. Next, she noticed the cloud of grey smoke billowing into the air and guessed that Blaine had fired up the grill. Now Jill was most likely chatting his ear off while he barbequed.

At least he hadn't cooked up his three-alarm chili. Krissy killed the engine. Grabbing her purse, she climbed out of the vehicle.

As she strode toward her husband and neighbor, Krissy experienced a twinge of guilt for not feeling more friendly. She supposed she should have compassion on the poor woman since Jill was terribly discouraged in her marriage. On the other hand, Krissy was tired, and she and Blaine were experiencing their own issues right now.

"Hey, you're home." A smile split Blaine's tanned face. "I didn't even hear you pull in." His gaze flittered to Jill in explanation, and Krissy understood immediately.

"I was just telling Blaine about Ryan's new work schedule. He's gone twelve, sometimes thirteen hours a day. When he comes home, he's so crabby, the kids and I can't stand to be around him. Worse, he expects dinner on the table and the house to be spotless."

"I told Jill I can relate since that's what you expect too, right, hon?"

Krissy rolled her eyes. "You haven't done housework in twenty years, Blaine."

"With three women around, why should I?" Pointing the metal spatula at her, he added, "And you haven't changed a flat tire in all that time. Or shoveled snow."

"You won't let me use your snow-thrower, otherwise I would." Krissy leaned into Jill. "This argument could go on all night."

The younger woman giggled. "I'm so glad to see you two aren't perfect. You seem like it sometimes. I'm really envious of your relationship." She peered into Krissy's face with teary brown eyes. "You don't know how lucky you've got it, girlfriend."

"I remind Krissy of that at least three times a day," Blaine said.

Sudden shouts from the adjoining back yard brought Jill to attention. "Uh-oh...sounds like Grant and Royce are at it again. I'd better scoot. Talk to you guys later."

"See ya, Jill," Blaine replied.

"Bye." Krissy watched their neighbor jog around the house before looking back at Blaine. "Hi."

"Hi." He stepped away from the smoking grill and gave her a kiss. "Have a good day?"

"Yeah, and you?"

"Okay."

"What did the doctor say?"

"He wants me to go back and see Dr. Klevins."

"The surgeon? How come?"

126

"Because my back isn't improving at the rate he'd like."

Krissy nibbled her lower lip in momentary contemplation. "Do you think another operation is ahead of you?"

"I doubt it. I've had a fusion. What more can the surgeon do?"

"I don't know."

Blaine stared at whatever he was cooking.

"What are you making for supper?" Krissy stood on tiptoes to peer into the grill.

Bringing his gaze back to hers, he grinned. "Beef tenderloin. One of your favorites."

The news made her smile. "I've been hungry for a grilled steak. And here I assumed you'd concocted your famous chili."

"You hate my chili. Why would I make it when it's only you and me for supper tonight?"

"Well, I—"

"See, I know you, Krissy. Better than you think." He raised an eyebrow as if to make his point.

"Touché." Hiking her purse strap higher onto her shoulder, she couldn't help smiling. "I'm going inside to change."

"Slipping into something more comfortable, are you, darling?" Blaine asked in a feigned British accent.

"Oh, like right." Krissy shook her head at him and walked to the side door. "I've got a mountain of things to accomplish tonight."

Entering the house, a swell of disappointment rose inside of her. She could sure use a romantic evening. Much to her shame, a vision of Matt Sawyer and his tender blue eyes flittered across her mind.

❦

"You're not eating."

Krissy glanced up from her plate. "Everything is perfect, Blaine. The steak, the salad, the dinner rolls..."

"But?"

"But I feel a little down all of a sudden. I can't explain it. It's weird."

"Maybe it's the company," Blaine quipped, setting his fork down none-too-gently.

Krissy stared at him ruefully. How could she make him understand what was going on in her heart when she didn't understand it herself? "Blaine..."

"You know what?" His dusky blue eyes held and earnest light, "I've been in love with you since we were juniors in high school."

Krissy smiled, eyes misty, as mental snapshots of the past scampered across her mind. "I know..."

"And when you agreed to go to the prom with me that year, I felt like the luckiest guy alive. I mean, Krissy Marens...*the* Krissy Marens, prettiest girl in school...agreeing to attend the event with me. And I wasn't even on the football team."

Laughing, she sat back in her chair and folded her hands in her lap. "I thought you were awfully cute."

Blaine's smile faded. "Change your mind lately?"

"No! What I meant was..." She sighed. "Oh, I don't know..."

She began picking at her salad again, not willing to see the pain she'd probably inflicted on the man she was supposed to love unconditionally. More guilt assailed her, although she'd made an attempt at honesty. Perhaps it would be better if she'd stuffed these feelings in the deepest part of her and somehow tried to forget them there.

"I can't help it that my hair is thinning," Blaine said. "This bald patch on the back of my head seems to get bigger every year."

Krissy glanced at him and smiled. "I like your bald spot. And I think your thinning hair makes you appear...distinguished."

"Hm..." He rubbed his jaw, looking perplexed. "Maybe my five o'clock shadow bugs you, is that it?"

"No, I like your five o'clock shadow. I wish it stuck around all day."

"Want me to quit shaving?"

Krissy rolled her eyes. "No." She laughed.

"Help me out here, woman," Blaine cried in exasperation, holding his arms out wide. "I want to please you, but how can I when I have no clue what's displeasing you?"

"The paunch hanging over your belt turns me off. There. I said it."

"Thank you." Throwing his gaze upward, he shook his head. "For your information, I plan to get rid of my...paunch...just as soon as my back heals up."

"That's what I figured, so I didn't want to make a big deal out of it. But you've been wearing such sloppy clothes lately."

"My blue jeans are a little snug. Besides, they're hard to pull on with my back killing me half the time."

Krissy shrugged and nodded simultaneously. She understood.

"Okay, okay, okay," he said, his palms out as if to forestall further debate. "I'll lose some weight. I'm not pleased with this extra twenty pounds either."

"You'll feel better, too. That's twenty pounds off your aching back."

Blaine humbly agreed. "Now, I need to ask you something else." He stood and took his silverware and half-empty plate to the sink. "Something important."

Krissy felt horrible for ruining his dinner. "What's the question?"

"I want a totally honest answer. No beating around the bush." After depositing his dishes near the sink, he turned and faced her.

She rose and cleared her place, setting everything on the counter next to Blaine's utensils. Standing in front of him, she gazed into his eyes, unsure if she trusted herself to be as forthright as he requested.

"You still love me, Krissy?" He looked almost vulnerable.

"Yes, I love you. Of course I love you. It's just that..."

"What?"

"It's just that in so many ways, Blaine, we're strangers."

"That makes no sense. We've been married for over twenty years. We've known each other since high school. How can we possibly be strangers?"

"Because since the twins were born, we put all our energy into raising them. We did a good job, too. But, when the girls were in first grade, I went back to school and finished my degree, and from that point on, I had my career, you had yours, and our home life consisted of our daughters and maintaining a house and paying bills."

Krissy expelled a long breath, hoping she was getting through to him. "I don't regret any of the sacrifices we made for Mandy and Laina, except for one. Our relationship. We lost touch, you and I, and now there's a distance between us that I'm unsure how to bridge."

Working the side of his lip between his teeth, Blaine seemed to be considering everything she said. He sighed, shrugged, and gathered Krissy into his arms. "If we love each other, which we do," he stated at last, "then we can pray about these things and work on spanning whatever gap exists."

Resting her head against the lower part of his shoulder, Krissy heard the strong, steady beat of Blaine's heart. She could smell smoke on his t-shirt from the outside grill. It was a scent she'd become well acquainted with over the years because of his occupation. She associated the odor with an unsettled sensation, and realized that even though they'd grown apart, she'd always concerned herself with his safety. She'd fretted and prayed for him during those hours following his accident. Wasn't that love? Of course it was.

Blaine placed a light kiss on her forehead. "Everything'll be all right."

She nodded and tightened her arms around his waist. "Fall always seems like a time of change and adjustment. A different school year, new students—and this year another school altogether for me, and now Mandy and Laina are gone."

"Honey, they're not 'gone.' You make it sound like they're dead. They're only away at college. It's a temporary thing."

"Like the season."

"Right. Life's full of seasons."

Krissy nodded, wishing this one would pass quickly.

# Six

IT WAS THE last day of the week and first day of September. Warm sunshine spilled through the partially cloudy sky and onto the black asphalt where Krissy's third graders were at play. Shiny new equipment in bright yellows and reds beckoned children of all ages to its monkey bars, slide, and swings. The little girl inside Krissy was tempted to join the kids each time she heard their squeals of laughter.

"I wish they would have made gym sets like that when I was growing up," fellow teacher, Erin Latrell, said. She stood to Krissy's right, observing her second graders.

Krissy laughed. "I was thinking along those same lines." Tipping her head, she considered the young lady. Krissy guessed Erin wasn't much older than the twins, with her peaches and cream complexion and blue-eyed innocence framed with shoulder-length, reddish-brown hair that fell in soft curls past her shoulders. "Mind if I ask where you attended college?"

"Not at all. I stayed right here in Wisconsin and lived with my folks. Still do, but I'm getting married soon. Next summer, in fact."

"How nice." Krissy smiled, wishing she'd insisted that Mandy and Laina lived at home while going to school. But, as she mentally replayed the conversation she'd had with each of her daughters, she realized they were happy and enjoying campus life. Besides, they truly needed this time to blossom and grow into godly, independent women.

Wistfully, she returned her gaze to the children at play. Blaine was right. *This is merely a season...a stormy one. And it's storming in my heart.*

The sound of hard sole shoes tapping against the pavement drew Krissy out of her reverie. Glancing over her shoulder, she saw Matt Sawyer, dressed in a light brown suit, striding towards them. Reaching Erin and her, he smiled.

"Nice day."

Krissy grinned politely. "It certainly is."

Erin nodded in agreement.

"I wanted to deliver these personally." He handed them both a white, sealed envelope. "They're invitations to my annual Labor Day party this coming weekend. Time got away from me, and I didn't trust placing them in teachers' in-boxes." He paused, bestowing a warm smile on Erin, then Krissy. "I'd be honored if you would both attend."

Krissy glanced down at the envelope in her hand, not wanting to look up into Matt's blue eyes. She was a married woman and to flirt would be very wrong, but if she wasn't mistaken, Matt sought out her company...and Krissy felt more than flattered. Worse, she enjoyed it.

*Oh, Lord, this is a bad situation, one I can't give into even if I'm tempted to...*

"May I bring my fiancé?" Erin asked.

"Of course. I'd love to meet him," Matt replied graciously. "And, Kristin," he added, turning toward her, "I hope you'll bring your spouse."

Why did that just sound like a question? Did Matt care one way or the other?

Pushing her ponderings aside, she tried to attack the issue pragmatically. Would she ask Blaine to come along? Or rather, would he deign to accompany her? In all probability, he'd elect to stay home. He abhorred attending social functions that included Krissy's coworkers. He said teachers were boring and one-upped each other as proof of their intellect. Of course, the same could not be said for Blaine's colleagues, who played tug-of-war over mud pits and blasted each other with fire hoses at their company picnics. Over the years, Krissy had attended each and every one with Blaine, and she did so without complaint.

Mustering her courage, she glanced up at Matt and gave him a formal smile. "I'll pass the invitation on to my husband. Thanks."

"Great," he said, but Krissy sensed the answer lacked Matt's usual enthusiasm.

As he walked away and reentered the school, her heart took a plunge from the weight of the guilt she'd been carrying around for almost two weeks. Yet she hadn't done anything to be ashamed about, except entertain thoughts of impossibilities. She wasn't about to leave Blaine in order to have a fling with her new principal. She was a Christian. She loved her husband. He loved her.

Krissy sighed. So what in the world was her problem?

❧

Blaine wasn't sure how he felt as he drove home that Friday afternoon. Disappointed, scared, and irritated all at the same time.

He'd seen the orthopedic surgeon and, after hearing the bad news, he'd checked in at the fire station to say hello to the guys. Next, he conversed with the captain for a long while, and, at last, Blaine saw the wisdom behind taking the permanent disability the city offered, along with a compensation package the union had procured for him. The surgeon stated that Blaine would never return to work. His back wasn't ever going to be as limber and as strong as it was before the accident. However, his physician ordered him to swim and lose weight—that is if he didn't want to turn into a mass of plump vegetation. So Blaine's next visit was to the local health club where he purchased a membership. He figured a work-out would use up an hour or two, but how would he spend the rest of his days?

*Lord, there has to be a job out there somewhere that I can do. A man doesn't work, he doesn't eat...*

Blaine pulled into the driveway and parked behind Krissy's minivan. He climbed out of his truck and entered the house. The aroma of sautéing garlic immediately met his senses. He followed his nose to the kitchen and found Krissy at the stove.

"Smells great in here." He placed his hands on her slim hips and kissed her neck. "What are you making?"

"A stir fry...with real chicken," she replied emphatically.

Blaine chuckled. "Your version of Chinese food is always tasty, hon. It's the order-out stuff that rouses my curiosity."

She turned. "What did the doctor say?"

Blaine recognized that no-nonsense tone. He chewed the side of his lip and considered her. Was she in one of her moods again? She hadn't even acknowledged the compliment he'd just paid her.

She tipped her head to one side. "Well?"

"I've got six months to live."

Krissy gave him a quelling look. "Don't even joke about such things, Blaine."

"Well, maybe that's what you'd like to hear," he blurted. He was getting tired of catering to her whimsical ups and downs. Didn't she care a whit about him?

Setting down the spatula, she faced him, hands on hips. "I'm not up to sparring with you, so just tell me what the doctor said, okay?"

Blaine exhaled and fought against the frustration welling inside of him. "He said I can't go back to work because I'll never be able to function in the capacity the fire department expects. So I stopped by the station and accepted the permanent disability offer and comp package. I'm no longer a firefighter."

Krissy's jaw dropped slightly. "You're out of a job? Just like that? Can't they give you some more time to recuperate?"

"It's been three months, Kris."

"But—"

"Look, the doc said it and my captain agreed. I can't physically perform my job safely and effectively. I'm done."

Krissy swallowed hard. "We can't live on my salary...and help put the girls through college."

"I'll have money coming in through my disability insurance. And I plan to find something else to do besides sit around here all day watching soap operas."

"You've been watching the soaps?"

Blaine laughed at Krissy's horrified expression. "I meant that figuratively."

She nodded, looking relieved, and began slicing the boneless chicken breasts and adding the pieces to the oil and garlic

"Honey, don't worry. Things are going to be fine. God will take care of us. He'll find me some sort of work that I can do to supplement my income."

"Yes, I...I'm sure He will."

Blaine folded his arms and watched his wife prepare their meal with lackluster efforts. It just wasn't like her. Up until a few weeks ago, she'd possessed an unsurpassed zest for life, but now, a kind of dreariness clouded her eyes. He wished he could get inside her head for five minutes. Maybe then he could understand whatever it was that bothered her...other than what she'd previously admitted to. He sensed the problem was more than his extra poundage and the girls being away at college, although the combination might have been the boiling point.

"Hard day at school, Kris?"

"Not exactly."

"Well, what *exactly* is bugging you right now? Me?"

"No...not you. It's just that I was thinking about quitting my job until you came home with your news."

Blaine brought his chin back in surprise. "Why do you want to quit your job? You don't like the new school?"

"I don't know...maybe I'm tired of teaching altogether. Maybe I've lost what it takes to be a good educator."

"That's not what you said Monday night. You said the kids adored you and that they were excited about their new third grade teacher. I really thought you were starting to snap out of this fog or depression...or whatever you want to call it."

Krissy began chopping celery, onions, and mushrooms. Next, she tossed the vegetables into the wok on the stove. "There's a certain person at school who..." She swallowed, and Blaine could tell she tried to select her words carefully. "Well, I don't know if it's...healthy for me to work near this person."

Blaine frowned. "Not healthy?"

"Emotionally speaking."

"Hm..." He thought it over. "So this person is verbally abusive or threatening?"

"Threatening...in a way."

"You're kidding? This person is making threats? Let's call the cops."

"No, no, Blaine, not that kind of threatening. I mean, he's not threatening me, he's just a threat to me."

"Like he wants to take over your job?"

Krissy turned thoughtful. "Something like that, I guess. He wants to take over something."

"Man, you wouldn't think that kind of competition existed in Christian day schools, but I suppose it's everywhere." He paused, thinking it over. "Listen, Kris, if after bathing the matter in prayer, you need to quit, go ahead. You'll find another position. Probably a better paying one, too." With that, he closed the distance between them and kissed her cheek. "See? Problem solved."

⚮

Krissy watched her husband's retreating form as he left the kitchen and entered the living room. Next, she heard the rustling of the paper and knew he'd taken to reading the daily local news.

Blaine thought the problem was solved. Far from it. Krissy jabbed at the stir-fry with the wooden spatula. Then she covered the top of the wok and allowed it to cook.

What could she say to make Blaine understand? Did she tell him she'd grown bored with their marriage and developed an attraction to Matt Sawyer? Krissy shook her head. Blaine would hit the ceiling. What husband wouldn't?

And here she was supposed to be a good, Christian wife.

Her spirit plummeted deeper with discouragement and shame. Not only was she a lousy wife, but she was a sorry excuse for a Christian woman too.

# *Seven*

KRISSY MOPED AROUND the house for the rest of the evening, and Blaine let her. Frankly, he didn't know what more to do for her, other than leave her alone and allow her to come to her own conclusions about whether she should quit her job. Meanwhile, Blaine started swimming on Saturday morning, and after completing several laps, he could tell the exercise would strengthen his back muscles. Maybe he'd take off this extra weight quicker than he anticipated. The idea encouraged him.

On Sunday morning, he and Krissy attended their usual Bible study and the service that followed. When the pastor gave an altar call, Krissy went forward, her expression more miserable than Blaine had ever seen it.

Helplessness caused him to step awkwardly into the aisle to allow Krissy back into the pew after she'd knelt and prayed silently up front. It comforted Blaine that she, at least, communed with their Heavenly Father. God held the answers that Blaine lacked, and the Lord would guide Krissy's decisions.

Back at home, she seemed...happier.

"Everything okay?" Blaine asked as they stood in their bedroom. He unknotted his tie then yanked it out from around his neck.

Krissy smiled and nodded as she changed her clothes. "Everything's fine."

"What do you want to do this afternoon?"

She stopped and glanced at him, her expression one of surprise. "You want to do something?"

"Yeah. Why is that such a shock?"

Krissy laughed softly and hung up her dress. "Because you usually want a nap on Sunday afternoons."

"That's when I was a hard-working man. Now I'm foot-loose and fancy-free."

"Oh, brother!" She sent a glance upward.

Blaine chuckled. "And tomorrow's a holiday, so you don't need a nap either."

"We sound like two old fogies."

"We are two old fogies. So what do you want to do this afternoon, *Granny*?" Judging from her wounded expression, Blaine instantly knew he'd said the wrong thing. "Honey, I was only kidding. The granny-thing was supposed to be funny."

"I know...I guess it just struck me hard." She gave him an earnest stare. "I'm not ready for old age."

"We're not getting any younger, Kris. I mean, think about it. We could be grandparents in the next couple of years."

"Bite your tongue!"

Blaine chuckled at her incredulous expression.

Krissy threw one of the bed pillows at him. He caught it and whipped it back, hitting her in the shoulder.

"All right, that's it. The war's on."

"Now, wait a second, here. I've got a bad back, remember?"

141

"Too bad. All's fair in love, war, and pillow fights."

Blaine grinned broadly. Krissy hadn't acted this feisty in months. Clad in her lacy slip, she made a fetching sight as she gathered her ammunition.

Her cell phone jangled with a popular Christian song, intruding upon their delightful moment.

"Don't answer it," Blaine said.

A grown creased Krissy's brow. "But it might be the girls."

He thought it over. "We'll call them back."

She chewed the side of her lip, the phone clamoring for her attention. Blaine figured he'd answer it for her and put her mind at ease. Lifting the device off her dresser, he pressed the talk button.

"Robinsons'."

"Um…I'm looking for Kristin. May I speak with her?" the male voice at the other end asked.

"Who's calling?"

"Matt Sawyer. I'm the principal of Heritage Academy."

"Oh, right. Sure. Hang on a sec." Using the mute feature, Blaine held the phone out for her. "For you."

"One of the girls?" She moved off the bed.

"Your new principal."

Blaine watched as Krissy paled in one second and blushed in the next. In fact, she turned scarlet right down to her collarbone. He narrowed his gaze, trying to gauge the odd reaction.

"What does he want?"

"Beats me," Blaine replied. "Should I tell him we're, um, busy?"

Krissy nodded, looking almost afraid to take the call.

Blaine took the call off mute. "Sorry, but Krissy's unavailable. Can I give her a message?"

"Yes, please. Ask her if she'd mind bringing a pan of brownies to the picnic tomorrow. My caterer's mother took suddenly ill, so I'm trying to put together an impromptu pot-luck."

Blaine pursed his lips and glanced at Krissy who was staring back at him curiously. "Sure, I'll ask her."

"If there's a problem, tell her to give me a call. She's got my number."

*She does?* Blaine swallowed a tart reply. Of course she would have his number stored. He was her boss. Nonetheless, there was something in the guy's tone he didn't appreciate. "Okay, I'll relay the message."

"Great. Thanks."

Blaine disconnected the call with his thumb. "Who's this Matt Sawyer anyway?"

⌡⌠

Krissy felt as though a hot blade pierced her gut. She placed her hand over her stomach, but reminded herself she'd done nothing to be ashamed of. "Matt's the principal of Heritage Academy."

"Yeah, that's what he said. And he wants you to make a pan of brownies for tomorrow's picnic. Did I know about this picnic?"

"No, because I wasn't planning to go."

"Hm...well, you'd better call the guy back and tell him. He said you've got his phone number."

Krissy frowned. Did she have his number here at home? Maybe on the picnic invite—except she'd tossed it out. But then she remembered... "It's in the staff directory."

"Why do you look so guilty, Kris?"

She shrugged. "Do I look guilty? I shouldn't. I didn't do anything wrong."

Blaine sat on the edge of the bed. "Is this guy hitting on you or something?"

Krissy shook her head and glanced at the printed bedspread. The last thing she wanted to do was discuss Matt Sawyer with her husband.

"He's not the one threatening you and making you feel like quitting your job, is he?"

"Matt isn't threatening me, no." How could she possibly describe the kind of "threat" the man posed? Matt walked into her classroom and she suddenly felt sixteen again, all weak-kneed and nervous. When he sought out her company, she was flattered, honored. They shared many common interests, and Krissy sensed the mutual attraction. Still, he knew she was married. So what was Matt thinking? The same thing she was thinking? That if she weren't espoused, they might have a chance at a relationship?

But the fact remained—she was married. Very married...and Krissy planned to stay that way, despite her wayward emotions.

Blaine cupped her chin, bringing her gaze up to his. "Everything okay?"

"Yes." Wasn't it? She felt so troubled in her heart, disquieted within her soul. Hadn't she gotten all this settled during the worship service?

"All right. If you tell me things are okay, then they are."

Krissy forced a little smile before Blaine leaned over and touched his lips to hers. It was like instant salve on a painful red welt, and she closed her eyes in sweet familiarity. She and Blaine were a perfect match. They fit together like hand-in-glove. One flesh.

He ended the kiss sooner than Krissy would have liked. "You never answered my question," he said, wearing a silly smirk. "What do you want to do this afternoon?"

Krissy grinned as her hand clutched the corner of a pillow, and before he could duck, she whacked him upside the head.

# *Eight*

KRISSY LEAFED THROUGH the staff directory, found Matt's phone number, then pressed in the number. Before she could connect, however, Blaine came up behind her and stole the phone out of her hand.

"Hey, I've been thinking...why don't we go to this picnic tomorrow?"

Krissy dropped her jaw. "You? Want to go to a picnic? With a bunch of teachers and their spouses?" She held her hand over her heart, feigning cardiac arrest.

He shook his head. "You'd starve to death if you went into acting."

She shrugged.

"But I'm serious. Maybe we should go. I mean, it's your new school and you're debating whether God wants you there...perhaps He'll show you at tomorrow's picnic."

*Nice try*, Krissy wanted to say. She wasn't that dumb. The reason behind Blaine's interest in attending was solely based on his curiosity about Matt. She likened it to the times she and the girls would return from an afternoon of shopping and Blaine would ask, "How much money did you spend?" to which Krissy replied, "Not much." Then Blaine would say, "Lemme see the checkbook." It wasn't that he didn't believe her or didn't trust her. He did, and he'd made that much clear over the years. He simply wanted to see the facts for himself. And in all probability, the same held true now with the principal of Wellsprings Academy. Obviously, Krissy hadn't adequately hid her tumultuous emotions when Matt phoned earlier. Now, Blaine wanted to appraise the situation for himself. Unfortunately, the idea of Blaine and Matt meeting made Krissy terribly uncomfortable.

"Blaine, I don't want to attend this picnic."

"Free food. You don't have to cook...except for a pan of brownies."

"I'll make you your own personal pan," she promised. "And I'll make your favorite cream cheese brownies, but only if we can stay home."

"Sorry, babe, I'm on a diet." He patted his tummy for emphasis. "Besides, you accused me of not enjoying the same things you do, so here's our chance to do something together. Something you enjoy."

Krissy inhaled deeply then let out a slow breath.

Blaine tipped his head. "Want to tell me why you're so dead-set against going to this little shindig?"

She considered his question. It would be nice to clear the air. But, at the same time, she didn't want to hurt Blaine by admitting her attraction to another man. Would he ever trust her again?

"Don't you think I'll understand?" His expression was soft, earnest.

"No, I don't think you will."

"Well, why don't you try me and see?"

"Because I don't want to take the chance. Besides, whatever I'm going through is something very personal. It's between God and me."

Blaine folded his arms. "I feel kinda left out."

She tried to ignore his pained expression. "Want to go to the zoo this afternoon?" She purposely changed the subject.

"Not particularly."

"I thought maybe we could even ask Jill if we could take her kids. You know, get them out of the house for a while so she and Ryan can spend some time alone."

Blaine grimaced. "I'd rather go to fifty school picnics than take a bunch of whining kids to the zoo."

"Oh, come on, Blaine, it'll be fun."

He puffed out an exasperated sigh. "How'd you manage to come up with this harebrained scheme?"

"Harebrained? Thanks a lot."

"The idea, not you, Krissy."

She folded her arms, trying to stifle her irritation. "For your information, I listened to Jill and Ryan argue at one o'clock this morning. They were in their kitchen with the window open, and they woke me up. I couldn't fall back asleep, and I started thinking about how we could help them. We can't enroll them in Christian marital counseling or a Bible study because they're opposed to anything religious. But during the worship service, I came up with...with this *harebrained scheme* of taking their kids to the zoo. It's a way to reach out to our neighbors."

"The zoo, huh?"

Krissy nodded.

Blaine rubbed his stubbly jaw in consideration then finally shrugged. "Okay, I'll go to the zoo this afternoon, but only if we can go to the picnic tomorrow."

"I'll think about it. I mean, I can always phone Matt later with our regrets."

Blaine shook his head. "No picnic. No zoo. I drive a hard bargain."

Jaw clenched, Krissy glared at him. Blaine stared right back. She could see the spark of determination in his dusky eyes. Against her better judgment, she relented. "Oh, all right. We'll go to the picnic. But I don't want to hear one complaint about you being bored."

He grinned wryly. "Got it."

"And you don't have to tell every stupid joke you know and embarrass me."

"Me? Tell stupid jokes? C'mon, hon, my jokes are always hilarious."

"Yeah, right." Spinning on her heel, she marched toward the front door. "I'll go ask Jill if we can take the kids this afternoon."

"Sure. And I'll be here on my knees praying she says no."

⸎

Happiness abounded in Krissy after Jill agreed to allow her four children to go on the zoo outing. In addition, Jill promised to spend some quality time with Ryan.

"I'm sorry we disturbed you last night," she muttered with an embarrassed expression.

Krissy gave the woman a warm smile." I wasn't so much disturbed as concerned, and I hope you don't think I'm a nosy neighbor trying to butt into your business."

"Are you kidding? You're a godsend. With the kids out of the way for a while, I might even accomplish a thing or two around the house, and that'll make Ryan happy. He's forever complaining about the messes. But I don't have any time to clean."

Krissy thought Ryan had better lighten up. But then she reminded herself that there are two sides to every situation, and she didn't know the other half of this one.

Sitting on a step in the back hall, she helped baby Haden put on his shoes. Once finished, she lifted him into her arms. He was about the cutest thing she'd ever seen with his blond curls and deep, brown eyes.

"Wanna go to the zoo?" she asked the eighteen month old.

"Zoo...Mama..." He pointed at Jill, and Krissy wondered if he'd cry when she took him home.

"Don't worry," Jill said as if divining her thoughts. "Haden will go anywhere with anyone– especially if his brothers and sister are along."

"Okay, then let's go." Krissy carried the youngest on one hip while the three other kids followed her back to her house.

"I guess I wasn't praying hard enough," Blaine mumbled when she entered.

"Hi, Mr. Robinson." The oldest added a cheery grin. At eight years old, he was a red-haired, freckle-face kid with a smile that displayed a future need for orthodontics. "You coming to the zoo with us?"

"Yep. Mrs. Robinson is making me."

"She is?" The boy gave her curious stare.

"He's teasing you, Grant." Krissy rewarded Blaine with a stony look.

He grinned back at her in reply.

"I like the aminals at the zoo," four-year-old Chelsea announced. Her coloring was similar to little Haden's. "I 'specially like the bears."

"I like the snakes," Royce interjected. The second oldest, his features were a mix of his siblings'. Reddish-brown hair framed inquisitive brown eyes with only a smattering of freckles.

"I like the snakes, too." Blaine grinned and pulled out his car keys. "Mrs. Robinson hates snakes, so we'll stay in that part of the zoo the longest."

"Yay!" the two older boys agreed.

"Oh, fine," Krissy retorted, "but then I'll make you all go to the gift shop where I'll shop for hours."

"Yay! We like the gift shop, too." Royce said.

Blaine laughed and headed out of the house. Krissy and the children trailed behind him. When they reached the van, the kids piled in, and Krissy converted one of the back passenger benches into a child's harnessed seat into which she strapped Haden. With the task completed, she made sure the others were belted in safely before she took her place up front.

Blaine gave her a sidelong glance from where he sat behind the wheel. "You sure you want to do this?"

"Too late now."

With a sigh of resignation, he started the engine and backed out of the driveway.

They arrived at the Milwaukee County Zoo, parked, and Blaine paid the admission fee, grumbling under his breath about the cost of four children and something about highway robbery. Krissy ignored the remarks. He was only half-serious anyway. They entered the gates with the children. The welcome sign proclaimed that this particular zoo was considered one of the finest in the country, and it housed approximately twenty-five hundred different animals. Krissy recalled fine times of bringing her third-grade class here on field trips. It was virtually impossible to see everything in a span of a couple hours.

Krissy got the kids' attention. "Okay, what animals should we visit first?"

"Can we ride the train?" Royce asked, and in the next moment, the calliope-like blare from the downsized steam locomotive heralded its arrival at the midget station.

The children were all in agreement. The train ride, which circled the zoo, must be their initial stop. Blaine murmured a little louder this time as he purchased the six tickets, although he seemed to enjoy the ride on this sunny September afternoon.

Krissy enjoyed it, too. Moreover, she relished holding a little one on her lap again. Her once-a-month nursery duty never completely satisfied the longing she'd harbored for years to have another child. Well, it obviously wasn't in God's plan. She'd have to wait for grandchildren.

After the train ride, they visited the polar bears and sea lions. Then it was on to the see the snakes and sundry other reptiles, all of which made Krissy's skin crawl. Next, the alligators, and they finally moved on to the monkey house.

"Now you boys'll feel right at home in here." Blaine chuckled as they entered the area where the chimps were swinging from tree limbs, jumping around, and picking at each other. "This reminds me of you guys playing on your gym set."

"Uh-uh," Grant said, an indignant frown furrowing his auburn brows. "We're not monkeys."

"It's a joke," Krissy assured the boy. "Mr. Robinson is always making bad jokes."

"Uh-uh," Blaine mimicked juvenilely.

"You're more trouble than these kids." She jabbed her elbow into his ribs.

"Oh, yeah?" He caught her arm and drew her tightly to his side. "Well, just for that little comment, you get to buy us all popcorn and soft drinks."

She shrugged, figuring it was the least she could do. Overall, Blaine was being a good sport.

A half-hour later, they sat on a park bench, munching on popcorn and watching the children who were preoccupied with the elephants.

"You know, that little guy is awfully cute." Blaine sent her a grin.

"Haden? Yes, he sure is."

"I used to often wish I had a son...not that I ever felt displeased about our twin daughters. But I prayed hard and long for a boy. Guess God answered that prayer with a 'no.'"

Shocked, Krissy stared at him. She had never guessed Blaine harbored such a desire all these years. He hadn't ever said anything. "We could have adopted. We still could, I suppose."

"Naw, I don't have the energy or the patience for kids anymore."

"You're out of practice."

"Yeah, maybe."

A rueful smile tugged at the corners of her lips while she studied Blaine's profile. Did he have any other regrets? The very question was evidence enough that she really didn't know this man the way she ought to.

*Two sides to every situation*, she thought, recalling her speck of wisdom concerning her neighbors. And in that moment, Krissy realized how one-sided, how self-focused she'd been. Blaine was hardly some amoeba, like the kind scaling the aquariums here at the zoo. He was man with emotions, ideas, feelings, and...disappointments.

"I'm sorry I couldn't give you a son." Krissy nearly choked on the words. "I would have loved one, too."

He glanced at her, and with his sunglasses hiding his eyes, she couldn't quite make out his expression. But if she guessed, she'd define it as surprise. "It's not your fault." He turned his line of vision back to the kids. "Just wasn't meant to be. I accepted that a long, long time ago."

*Acceptance.*

The word clung to Krissy's heart for the remainder of the afternoon.

# Nine

BLAINE GROANED AND stretched out on the sofa and placed his head in Krissy's lap. "I think I outdid myself at the zoo today. My back is killing me."

"Oh, I'm sorry," Krissy replied, feeling guilty for insisting they go. "Sometimes I forget you're recuperating."

"Sometimes I do, too, and therein lies the problem."

Smiling at the retort, she ran her fingertips through Blaine's chestnut-colored hair. Thick and coarse, he kept it cropped short and, despite his remarks about his bald spot, he still possessed quite a lot of hair around the sides and on top of his head.

"Blaine, can I ask you something?"

"Sure you can." He peered up at her expectantly.

"I've been thinking ever since you said you wished we'd had a son...well, do you have any...regrets?"

"Regrets about what? Our relationship or life in general?"

"Life in general."

"Sure. Who doesn't?"

Krissy grew more curious. "What do you regret?"

"Not becoming a Christian sooner in life for one thing. The girls were, what, in third grade or something when we accepted the Lord?"

She nodded, recalling how the twins had gone to Vacation Bible School one summer and how, at the closing program, she and Blaine heard the gospel for the first time. Neither had any trouble accepting the Word of God as truth. Each had been raised to revere the Bible and God. However, they'd trusted in something other than Jesus Christ for their salvation.

"On occasion, I think that if we'd known then what we know now..." He chuckled. "What's that old cliché? Hindsight is twenty-twenty vision?"

Krissy agreed. "What about our relationship, Blaine? Any regrets there?"

"None whatsoever. And you?"

"No..." She hedged slightly.

"That didn't sound very convincing, Kris."

Contrition filled her being. "Sorry. I'm a different person today with different interests, likes and dislikes. I'm not the same woman you married."

"Tell me one person who stays the same over twenty years' time." Blaine's stare intensified.

"But that's what I mean...if we had to do it all again, would we?"

"The question is hypothetical, Kris." His exasperation was evident in his voice. "The fact is, we can't do it all again, so why even bother speculating?"

"You're right."

"You know as well as I do that we can't change what's happened in the past. We can only go forward."

"True."

Krissy continued to caress his scalp, running a finger down the side of his face and around his ear. Blaine closed his eyes, appearing as though he might fall asleep. She wondered if he were right, that perhaps she had begun to dwell on things beyond her control...and imagine things she had no right thinking about, such as Matt Sawyer. Try as she might to rid her thoughts of the tall, broad-shouldered man with a sparkling blue gaze, it seemed impossible. Was she obsessed, or was this something that happened to people at one time or another during their marriage?

"Can I ask one more thing?'

"Shoot."

"In all the years we've been married, were you...well, did you ever find yourself attracted to another woman?"

Blaine cocked one eye open. "Nope."

"Oh, come on, you're a red-blooded man and you're not blind."

"True, but I don't allow myself any appreciative glances. It's like Pastor said one Sunday. The first look is accidental, the second look is sin." Blaine grinned. "On my life, Kris, I never needed to take a second look. I've got it too good at home."

His words should have comforted her, but instead they caused Krissy to feel even more guilty.

Blaine pushed himself into a half-sitting position and searched her face. "Are you feeling insecure about us? I mean, you don't think I'm doing something I shouldn't, do you? Was it because Jill came over that day I was grilling? Honestly, I wouldn't dream of—"

She placed her fingers over his lips. "The thought never even entered my mind. I trust you. Completely. The truth is I trust you more than I trust myself."

Confusion swept across his features. "What's that s'posed to mean?"

She swallowed. "I'm not sure how to explain it."

"Try." He narrowed his gaze. "Does it have something to do with your not wanting to go to this picnic tomorrow?"

"Yes."

Blaine paled but remained amazingly calm. "Tell me, Krissy," he whispered.

Tears filled her eyes. "I want to tell you, Blaine, because after today, I realize that I...I need your help."

"All right. Whatever you need, I'll give it to you."

"I'm afraid you'll hate me if I tell you. I hate myself."

Blaine swung his legs off the sofa and stood. He ambled to the large picture window on the far wall of their living room and gazed out across the lawn before turning back to Krissy, "Honey, I could never hate you. You're the love of my life."

Rising, she strolled slowly toward him, wiping a tear off her cheek. "You know I've been in this funk since the girls went away to college."

Blaine nodded.

"Well, then I began teaching at the Academy where I met...the principal, Matt Sawyer. Almost immediately, we discovered that we had common interests. What's more, Matt listened to me and validated my feelings, and he wasn't so macho that he couldn't share his...and he did."

"I figured it had something to do with him." Blaine bit his bottom lip as if struggling to keep his temper in check. "So how far did it go?" he heard himself ask.

"How far did what go?"

"The affair?"

Volcanic-like horror erupted inside of Krissy, and she was momentarily dumbstruck.

"You didn't have a fling with this guy? That's not what you're telling me?"

"No, Matt's never touched me."

"You gave me heart failure for nothing?"

"It's not nothing!" Krissy threw her hands in the air. "See, that's what you do. You make light of everything important to me. I'm torn in two over this. Doesn't that matter?"

"Of course it does. I'm not taking any of this in stride, and I'm determined to understand... except I don't."

Krissy sniffed back her tears. She'd have to be blunt. "I'm attracted to Matt. It isn't right and our friendship is inappropriate at best, but there's this part of me that enjoys his company...and it's evident he enjoys mine. That's why I don't want to attend the picnic tomorrow. I don't want to see him and be reminded of all these crazy things I feel—and I certainly don't want them to develop. You're my husband, Blaine, and I'm committed to our marriage no matter what. It's just that..."

"It's just that your heart isn't in it anymore," he finished for her.

Despite her shame, she managed to nod in silent affirmation.

Blaine's eyes grew misty. "I won't deny that your admission hurt. It did, but I imagined worse. Guess I'm grateful for your honesty." He stepped closer and set his hands on Krissy's shoulders. "But even if you confessed to a full-blown affair, I'd fight for our marriage. With God on my side, I would have won, too, or died trying."

"No doubt."

He pulled her into his arms. Her tears refused to stay in check. "You must be so angry with me."

"No, not angry..."

"I'm sorry, Blaine. I didn't want to t-tell you because I didn't w-want to h-hurt you."

"It's better that I know." He kissed the top of her head while she sobbed into his sweatshirt. "I'm glad you told me. I love you, Kris, and I want you to be happy." He pushed her back slightly and gazed into her eyes. "But I want your heart. It belongs to me and I want it back." With his thumb, Blaine gently brushed away the sadness, turmoil, and remorse streaming down her face.

"I want you to have my heart, too, Blaine."

"Your willingness is half the battle. Your honesty about this whole thing almost guarantees your victory,"

"You really think so?" Hope slowly dispelled her negative emotions.

"I know so." He pulled her close to him again, but Krissy sensed the battle had only just begun.

# *Ten*

THE NEXT MORNING, Krissy awoke to the children's laughter outside her bedroom window. It took a moment before she realized the kids next door were playing in their yard

With a yawn, Krissy rolled over and glanced at the alarm clock on the bedside table. Surprised, she lifted her head from the pillow and stared hard at the glowing numerals. Could it really be ten-thirty in the morning? She looked at the vacant place beside her and the obvious registered. Blaine was up already.

Climbing out from under the bedcovers, she strolled to her closet and pulled on her robe for warmth against the pervading chill. But since it was only September, Blaine wouldn't want to turn the heat on yet.

She stopped in the bathroom, freshened up, and brushed out her hair. Finally, she made her way to the kitchen where she found Blaine standing in front of the sink, holding a cup of coffee in his hands, and staring out the window.

"G'morning."

He turned around and gave her a small smile. "It's about time you wake up, lazybones."

Krissy scrunched her countenance in a sassy reply and walked toward him. "Any more coffee?"

"Uh-huh." He handed her a mug from the cupboard.

"Blaine," she began as she poured the fragrant dark brew from the carafe, "you haven't said much since our discussion yesterday afternoon. Does that mean you're upset?" Taking a sip of coffee, she turned to view his expression. It was thoughtful, serious.

"What guy wouldn't be upset?"

Krissy grimaced. "I know..."

"But like I said, I'm glad you told me. And I've given the matter a lot of thought. I didn't sleep much, and with every lap I swam this morning, I asked the Lord what I should do about the situation."

"And?"

"Well, first let me tell you what I *wanted* to do. I wanted to phone Sawyer and tell him that not only are we unable to attend his picnic today, but that you aren't returning to work tomorrow...or ever." He sighed. "It took every ounce of strength I had not to give into the urge. But the Lord showed me that I really need to trust you and let you decide how to handle this situation."

Krissy's heart warmed to his words. "I've got good news for you. I'm not going back to the Academy. I decided that much already. I'll call Matt today and let him know, and I can clean out my desk tomorrow morning before school starts." She paused, encouraged to see relief on Blaine's face. "But I want you to know that I could probably face anything now, knowing that you're praying me through it." She took a step closer. "With you and God on my side, I can do anything."

Again just a hint of a smile. "I'm glad you're feeling better, hon."

"But you're angry, aren't you? I can sense it."

"Yeah, I'm angry...at him. The jerk." A muscle worked in Blaine's jaw. "He knew all along you're married. He should have kept his distance."

"I'm not exactly innocent. I should have kept my distance, too."

"True, but I've got a hunch that guy might have enjoyed busting up our marriage."

Krissy didn't agree. She rather thought Matt had fallen into the situation just as she had. It wasn't a premeditated thing. The attraction, the chemistry between them, was palpable from the beginning.

"Listen, I'm a man, so I know how men think. The thrill of a conquest and all that. But as a Christian, Sawyer should never have befriended you. I mean, if I sensed a woman was attracted to me, I wouldn't go out of my way to discover all the great things she and I had in common."

Mulling it over, Krissy admitted Blaine made a good point. She took another sip of coffee and recalled the many times Matt had sought out her company. She'd rationalized it away, feeling badly for him because of what he'd gone through with his wife. She had thought he merely wanted someone to talk to—a comrade. However, she'd mistakenly opened her heart to him when her heart belonged to Blaine.

Krissy shut her eyes and anguished over this whole mess. "I'm so sorry." Raw and renewed emotion threatened to choke her. "Can you ever forgive me? Can you ever trust me again?"

"I can, yes, on both accounts."

She peered tearfully yet gratefully into her black coffee. "But it'll take time, won't it?" When Blaine didn't answer, she glanced at him.

"It's going to take more than time, Kris." His grey eyes darkened. "It's going to take patience, communication on both our parts, commitment to our relationship, and...last but hardly least, it's going to take a lot of love."

Krissy felt oddly impressed by his answer. It sounded rehearsed, but that only meant he'd really been giving the matter his utmost attention. Finally, he took her, and her thoughts and feelings, seriously.

"I'm willing." She set down her mug on the counter. She slipped her arms around Blaine's mid-section and smiled despite her misty gaze. "I do love you. And I think you're pretty terrific to put up with me."

He set his forearms on her shoulders, coffee cup still in hand. "And I think you're pretty...period."

She tipped her head, feeling both flattered and surprised. "You really think I'm still pretty?"

"No, actually I think our girls are pretty. You're...beautiful."

Her smile grew. "It's been a long time since you told me that."

"I tell you all the time."

"No, you don't."

"Well, I *think* it all the time."

Krissy shook her head. "Too bad I can't read your mind."

Obvious chagrin crept across his face. "Okay, so I should say what I'm thinking more often. I'll try."

"And that's all I can ask for."

He nodded. The pact was sealed. Then, as Blaine regarded her, a tender expression deepened the hue of his eyes. Slowly, he lowered his mouth to hers. On contact, she closed her eyes, deciding this was most pleasurable kiss he'd given her in a long while. Gentle, undemanding, yet heartfelt and sincere.

After several long moments, Blaine lifted his chin and kissed the tip of her nose then her forehead.

"You smell like chlorine," Krissy blurted.

"From the pool."

"Kind of a different smell for you." At his questioning frown, she added, "I'm used to you smelling like smoke."

"Those days are gone."

"And I'm glad. No more fretting over you fighting fires."

A wry grin curved the corners of Blaine's lips. "So now that we're both unemployed, what do you want to do with all the time we're going to have together?"

"The rest of our lives," she murmured. Funny how the thought didn't seem so oppressing anymore. She grinned up at him. "Blaine, I'm sure we'll think of some way to amuse ourselves."

❦

That night, Krissy watched Blaine stack kindling in the fireplace and light it. Then she glanced across the dimly lit room at their neighbors who sat together on the love seat, sipping hot cocoa, and she marveled at the turn of events this afternoon. Earlier, as Blaine manned his post at the grill, slopping thick barbeque sauce on fat spare ribs, Ryan had sauntered over and began complaining about wives, kids, and marriage in general. After a lengthy discussion, Blaine invited Ryan and Jill and their brood over for supper.

That was the first thing to blow Krissy's mind. Blaine always acted more irritated by the Nebhardts than concerned for them and their marriage.

The second thing that sent her reeling was when Blaine suggested the younger couple get a sitter and come over after their children were settled. Surely, he would have much preferred to plant himself in front of the television tonight rather than entertain Jill and Ryan.

But when Blaine sat down at the piano and began to play for their guests, Krissy's head really began to spin. She hadn't heard him play in years.

"I wrote this piece just after I left for college," he'd announced. "I hated leaving Krissy behind. So I composed this sonata. I called it "September Sonata." He grinned over his shoulder at his audience. "It was the very piece that made her say 'I do.'"

His fingertips danced across the ivory keys of the baby grand in the corner of their living room, and Krissy's face flamed with self-consciousness. The stirring melody evoked a host of memories that she disliked reliving in front of her neighbors. That sonata—an instrumental musical composition consisting of three or four movements – how like their relationship it seemed. From falling in love to their perfect wedding day, to becoming parents and watching their daughters mature into lovely young women, their song of life had now begun to play a tune of rediscovery.

Suddenly, their future together looked more than promising. It seemed downright exciting.

Krissy felt proud of Blaine, and the Nebhardts seemed impressed with his talent and applauded when he finished playing. His face reddened before he announced he'd make a fire.

Brushing the wood dust from his hands now, Blaine walked over and claimed his place beside Krissy on the couch. It may have been her imagination, but she thought his blue jeans fit a little better, and instead of wearing one of his usual, worn out sweatshirts, he wore a dark-gray pullover, which he had neatly tucked into his pants. Making himself comfy, he stretched his arm out around her shoulders.

"You guys are so cute together," Jill remarked. "Like newlyweds or something."

"Well, we are...kinda." Blaine sent Krissy a meaningful wink.

"So you survived raising kids, huh?" Ryan asked.

"Just barely." Blaine grinned at his quip, but an instant later, he turned serious. "If I've learned anything, it's that I need to cherish my wife." His gaze locking with Krissy's, he added, "If I ever lost her, I'd have nothing. I'd be nothing. I only wish I had realized it years ago. I wish I would have made time for her...for us...in spite of our hectic schedules."

There beside him, Krissy felt like her wanderlust heart found its way home. Blaine wasn't a man to make public professions, especially when they pertained to his personal life. He had sincerely meant every word he'd just spoken.

She glanced up at him in a measure of awe, and for the first time in years, she felt unmistakably loved—and, yes, even cherished.

# Epilogue

ICY FEAR GRIPPED Blaine Robinson's heart as he raced down the hospital corridor. He'd been conducting a routine insurance inspection for the company at which he'd been employed for the past year when he'd gotten Krissy's page. He had left right away, but was he too late?

A nurse in lime-green scrubs and a matching cap stepped into his path. "Can I help you, sir?"

"My wife," he panted, "her name is Krissy Robinson."

"Right this way."

Blaine followed the woman through a set of doors and down another hallway.

"If you want to go in with her, put a gown over your clothes."

"Fine." Blaine didn't care what he had to do. All he wanted was to be with Krissy.

The woman handed him a blue printed gown and he immediately pulled it on and tied it in the back of his neck.

"Ready? The nurse smiled.

"Ready as I'll ever be, I suppose."

"Aw, come on now," she said with a teasing smile, "you've got the easy job."

"Yeah, so I've been told."

She laughed and escorted him into the birthing room where Krissy reclined in a specialized delivery bed.

Blaine rushed to her side. "I got here as soon as I could." He noticed the beads of perspiration on her brow as he bent to kiss her forehead.

Krissy held out her hand, and he took it. "The contractions came on so fast."

"No kidding. You were fine this morning."

"I know..."

Her body suddenly compelled her to bear down hard, and she was helpless to do otherwise. A moment later, she collapsed against the back of the bed, letting go of the handgrips.

"All right, this is the big one," Dr. Herman announced, her soft voice carrying a note of excitement to Blaine's ears. Despite Krissy's routine ultrasound exams, they had decided against learning the sex of their unborn child. "Another push. That's it."

But this was the part he hated, those agonizing last few minutes. Standing by Krissy's side, he knew his "job" was to encourage her, except it was hard to get past the feeling of utter helplessness.

Krissy squeezed his hand and cried out in final travail before falling back against the bed again. Blaine brushed the hair from her face, and then the newborn's squall filled the room. Exhausted, Krissy went limp.

"I'm too old for this."

Blaine grinned at her quip and turned his gaze on the doctor with anticipation coursing through his veins. "Is it a he or another she?"

The woman's round face split into a smile. "It's definitely a he!"

"Are you sure?" After he'd spoken those words, Blaine felt like an idiot. The doctor's incredulous glare only confirmed it.

"Of course I'm sure."

"Don't mind him, Dr. Herman," Krissy said. "I think my husband is overwhelmed."

"To say the least." Blaine swallowed quickly. He took several quick swallows in order to keep his emotions in check. He and Krissy had prayed for a son ever since they'd discovered she was expecting. Now that God had answered their fervent request, Blaine could scarcely believe it. He'd never thought this day would come, and over the past seven months, he had found himself praying like the man in the Gospel of Mark. "Lord, I believe, help thou my unbelief."

One of the nurses placed the baby on Krissy's abdomen. She clamped the cord in two places, then offered the scissors to Blaine. He took it and cut the umbilical cord, feeling glad that the hospital staff allowed men to take such an active role in the birth of their children. He'd read everything he could find on the Internet pertaining to pregnancy and childbirth, he'd monitored Krissy's diet, and even attended the birthing classes with her. But now, he felt cheated because he'd arrived so late. He'd looked forward to assisting with the delivery.

However, his disappointment paled beside the joy surging inside of him. They had a son. Putting an arm around Krissy, he watched as she cradled him.

"I love you," he whispered in her ear.

"I love you, too." She placed one hand against Blaine's face. He kissed her palm. "This is one of the happiest moments of my life."

"Ditto."

Krissy smiled. "We have our little boy at last."

Blaine's eyes grew misty.

"And you know what else?"

"Hm…?"

"You're my very best friend, and I couldn't stand the thought of bringing our baby into the world without you by my side. I tried my best to hold back the labor, but I couldn't fight the inevitable for long."

"You did just great, and God saw fit to get me here in the nick of time." He gave her shoulder an affectionate squeeze. "And for the record, Kris, you're my best friend too. Want to know something else?"

"What?"

"It's going to stay that way, despite diapers, bottles, and frenzied schedules. Neither your daycare center nor my part-time job…nor our precious children…will come between us as long as I'm alive and have something to say about it."

Krissy smiled and glanced down their latest little blessing who dozed contentedly. Looking back at Blaine, she said, "That's a promise I'm going to hold you to."

"Good."

Several moments passed before Krissy spoke again. "This marks a whole new season of life for us. We've got a baby again."

"You're only realizing that now?" Despite his teasing, he got the message. God was still composing their life's sonata…

And this was simply the next interlude.

# Blaine's 3-Alarm Chili

Step 1

1 pound lean ground beef

Step 2

1 onion, chopped
1-24 oz. can of spicy pasta sauce
24 oz. water
1-14.5 oz. can of diced tomatoes
¼ cup salsa

Step 3

6 oz. spaghetti noodles, broken in approximately 1-inch pieces

Step 4

1-16 oz. chili beans, un-drained

Step 5

8 oz. shredded cheddar cheese.
8 oz. sour cream

Step 1: In a 6.5 quart Dutch oven, brown ground beef. Drain. Add ingredients in Step 2. Bring to a boil, then turn down the stove's burner to a low simmer and cook for 1 hour, stirring occasionally. Add spaghetti pieces (step 3) and simmer for ½ hour, stirring frequently. Add un-drained chili beans (step 4) and cook over lower heat for another ½ hour, stirring occasionally.

Serve in soup bowls and top with shredded cheddar cheese and a dollop of sour cream (step 5).

Serves 6-8

# Let It Snow

# *Dedication*

To my son Rick…
An awesome army veteran, flight paramedic,
Emergency room RN, and regional EMS director—
Most importantly a fabulous "daddy."
You're an incredible individual with a heart as big as the moon.
You are a true hero!

# *One*

"OH, THE WEATHER outside is frightful, but the fire is so delightful..."

Sharon Rose Flannering leaned forward and pushed her car stereo's button off. She always enjoyed singing along with the classic seasonal song, but the weather outside really was frightful tonight, and she needed to concentrate on her driving.

The wipers flapped from right to left in a futile attempt to keep the windshield free from snow. Visibility was next to nil. All Shari could see of the road before her was a blur of white.

"Lord, I know I said I missed snow on Christmas, but You didn't have to do exceeding, abundantly, and above all I asked in this circumstance."

In spite of the situation, Shari smiled. Through life's many trials, God had proved to her His word was truth. For Shari, Proverbs 17:22 rang especially factual. "A merry heart does good, like medicine." With everything she'd been though in the last ten years, she'd needed that *saving medicine*—laughter. Besides, God's remedy cost nothing compared to psychotherapy and antidepressants—the other options. Yes, smiling and laughing kept the joy alive in her heart. She felt happy. Life was good. God was in control.

Even in the midst of a Wisconsin blizzard like this one.

Shari's cell phone rang and she answered it without taking her eyes off the road as her car continued to creep along the Interstate. "Hello?"

"Where are you?" Her mother's voice held a note of concern.

"I'm not sure. I can't see anything."

"Oh, no...in that case, I've no clue what to tell you. We weren't supposed to get this storm until tomorrow."

Shari grinned. "I haven't been gone so long that I've forgotten Wisconsin's fickle weather."

"For the record, I voted to visit you in Florida this Christmas."

"We celebrate that way every year, Mom. And now with Greg gone..."

Shari didn't finish the sentence. No need to. Her husband of twenty-three years had suffered with brain cancer for nearly a decade, and Shari's family endured the emotional highs and lows of his illness right along with her. Surgeries and radiation treatments had once kept Greg's disease in check, but then the time came when doctors could do no more. Since Greg had known Jesus Christ in a personal way, Shari battled the urge to slide into sadness and depression. Instead, she rejoiced that God chose to deliver her husband from his terrible pain and perform the ultimate healing— taking Greg to heaven. But she still mourned him, still felt the loss, and this was her first Christmas without him. That was one of the reasons she'd elected to come home.

Home. Funny how Wisconsin still seemed like home even though she'd lived elsewhere for more than half her life.

Suddenly, red brake lights ahead shone through the swirling white snow and snapped Shari back to attention. A moment later, she rejoiced. "Mom, a salt truck is right in front of me. Isn't that awesome? I'll follow this monstrosity until I can figure out where I am. Then I'll call you back."

"Please be careful, honey. I'm so worried about you. I just knew you shouldn't have driven all the way from Pensacola."

"I'm fine. Don't fret."

Shari quelled her impatience with her mother. Sylvia Kretlow was a pastor's wife, and yet she couldn't scrape up enough faith to equal that of the "grain of a mustard seed," like Jesus spoke of in the Gospel of Matthew. She assumed the worst in all situations. Shari's dad, the minister, wasn't much better. He held a doom and gloom outlook on life, insisting he was "a realist" and "serious-minded." But his sober attitude caused him to keep a choking hold on Shari and her siblings during their teenage years, which only fueled their rebelliousness. If Shari hadn't run off with Greg Flannering at the age of twenty, she was convinced that coming to trust Christ as her Savior would have been an impossibility. As it was, her sister and two brothers still hadn't arrived at a saving knowledge of Him.

And that was another reason for her visit to Wisconsin. Shari hoped to be used as an instrument of God's love this holiday season, beginning tonight, Christmas Eve. Since Greg's death, Shari felt all the more determined to reach a lost and dying world with the Christmas story, starting with her siblings. Unfortunately, they'd heard the salvation message since birth. Words wouldn't reach them anymore. God needed to do something miraculous in order to reach Mark, Luke, and Abby.

"It seems like tragedies always happen during Christmastime," Mom lamented. "I don't want our family to suffer another loss this year. Greg's dying was hard enough."

Shari grinned. "Your optimism is ever so encouraging."

Mom clucked her tongue at the quip.

"Let me figure out where I am," Shari repeated, "and afterwards, I'll call you back."

"All right, but…please be careful."

"I will. I promise."

Shari disconnected the call and forced herself to relax. Following the enormous truck made driving a hundred times easier. However, ten miles later, the truck veered onto the off-ramp. Shari did the same, realizing only too late that she'd exited the Interstate. But then, just to her right, she saw a well-lit, green and white sign advertising the Stop 'n' Shop. She pulled into the gas station and convenience store, deciding this would be the perfect opportunity to find out her precise location.

Parking alongside a pump, grateful for the overhead protection from the storm, Shari filled her vehicle's gas tank before entering the shop. The clerk couldn't have been more than nineteen, and he chatted with three scraggy-looking young men who leaned on the counter, smoking cigarettes. They seemed harmless enough, although Shari wrinkled her nose at the noxious smell. She noticed the blue haze lingering over the counter-enclosed cash register area. To her relief, however, the rest of convenience store didn't seem smoky.

She visited the ladies' room, then returned to the checkout counter just as a country-western rendition of "Silent Night" resounded through the speakers.

"I'm just entering Green Bay?" Shari blinked in surprise after the clerk replied affirmatively to her question. It seemed like an eternity ago that she'd driven through Manitowoc. Under normal weather conditions, the drive between the two cities took about thirty minutes.

"Where you headed?" the ruddy-complexioned young man asked.

"Forest Ridge. It's a little town in Door County—on the other side of the bay."

"I'm aware of where it is." He finger-combed his tree bark-brown hair back off his forehead. "Wouldn't try to make it there tonight, though."

Shari frowned. "But it's Christmas Eve."

All four young men gave her sympathetic shrugs.

"There're a bunch of hotels on the west side of I-43," a guy with shaggy blond hair suggested. He blew a plume of smoke into the air. "You might want to stay at one of 'em."

"Yeah, snow's not s'posed to let up for a while," the clerk added.

Shari shook her head. "I want to be with my family. I've driven all the way up from Florida to spend the holidays with them."

"Should've arrived yesterday." The employee grinned. "It was forty degrees outside."

The exact thought had occurred to Shari at least a kazillion times while journeying through several long, uninteresting states. Still, she hadn't been able to get off work any earlier. She'd considered flying, but it wasn't her ideal mode of transportation. Driving, on the other hand, gave her time to think while she took in the beautiful scenery each state offered.

Back in her car, she phoned Mom. After a few minutes, Dad got on the line.

"You're near Miriam Sheppard's bed-and-breakfast. She calls it a 'highway haven,' and it stays open all year long. Why don't you call it a night and sleep there?"

"With the Sheppards?" Shari let go a peal of laughter. Stay with the Sheppards? No way! "I don't think so."

"Why not? Miriam asks about you all the time," Dad said. "She's probably alone tonight. Your mother's nodding her head and...what? Oh, Karan's at her in-laws' and Brenan is in...Africa. No, make that Brazil."

Shari was well aware of Brenan's whereabouts. Her church supported his missions team, and she read its quarterly newsletter. Dr. Brenan Sheppard had come a long way from the quiet, lanky guy Shari had dated through high school and two years into college. Back in those days, Brenan possessed about as much ambition as the young men inside the gas station, assuming that's all they wanted to do with their lives. While Shari didn't regret breaking off their engagement, she was sorry for the way in which she did it. An unkind, impersonal letter.

Then she ran off and eloped with Greg Flannering. At the time, Greg and his family were new to the area. Shari had met Greg at a nightclub. It was love at first sight for the both of them, even though Shari was engaged to Brenan.

Years later, after she committed her life to Christ, Shari wrote Brenan a much different letter and apologized. He never replied, and she didn't try to contact him again. But she'd heard he never married, and she always felt responsible—like the woman who irreparably broke the poor man's heart. So she prayed for him, asking God to bring about a wife for Brenan. But now, staying at his mother's bed-and-breakfast seemed a little intimidating, although Shari had always liked Miriam. The older woman was a widow too. Her husband had died years ago, and instead of moving back to Forest Ridge where she'd raised her children, Miriam continued to run the bed and breakfast, a small but profitable business that began after she and her husband retired.

But what a shame that Miriam wouldn't enjoy her family all gathered around her tonight, filling that big house of hers.

"She's alone, huh?"

"Shall I have your mother give Miriam a call?"

Gazing through her windshield, Shari felt like she'd been planted inside a snow-globe. At once, she saw the wisdom in not attempting the rest of the drive. "Yeah, go ahead. If worst comes to worst, I'll find a hotel."

"Okay, we'll call you right back.

Stepping out of her car again, Shari traipsed back into the Stop 'n' Shop. She purchased a cup of coffee and sat down at one of the four tables near the restrooms. As she sipped the too-strong brew, Shari was glad that she'd donned her comfy, wrinkle-free black knit dress and button-down red holiday sweater. She'd stayed overnight in Cincinnati and determined to drive straight through to Forest Ridge today. She should have made it in ten or eleven hours, including lunch and bathroom stops. She'd hoped to arrive in time for tonight's Christmas Eve service. She'd dressed for the occasion this morning before leaving the hotel, anticipating that she'd just make it. Too bad the weather decided not to cooperate with her plans.

Shari's smart phone rang with a melodious tune that alerted her to an incoming call. She answered it. "What took so long?"

"Oh, I'm sorry," Mom said. "Miriam and I got to chatting. Anyway, she said it's fine. She'd love for you to stay with her. She's got plenty of room in her bed and breakfast. It's not too far from the gas station you're at."

Shari listened carefully to the directions. The Open Door Inn couldn't be more than a mile away.

"Great, I'm off. I'll call you after I get settled." She tamped down the disappointment at not being with her family tonight. "Merry Christmas, Mom."

"Merry Christmas, honey. We'll see you tomorrow and celebrate then. At least I'll know you're safe tonight."

"Right. G'night."

Shari ended the call and shrugged back into her black wool coat. After wishing a Merry Christmas to the four young men still congregated around the checkout, she ventured back outside and into the winter wonderland.

⁓

"At forty-three years old you're finally getting married."

Brenan smiled at his sister, Karan Strong, as she shook her head covered with an abundance of silky, honey-blond hair. He enjoyed watching her stunned reaction to his news.

"I can't believe it."

"Well, I didn't pop the question yet. Elena could always turn me down."

Karan lowered herself onto the floral-upholstered settee. "Doesn't sound like she will."

Brenan didn't think so either. The slim, dark beauty he'd met in Brazil had gotten under his skin in the most unusual way. Had to be love. Elena said she loved him. The only drawback in his mind was the thirteen-year difference in their ages. It bothered him.

Brenan glanced at the doorway in time to watch his brother-in-law, Dan Strong, enter the living room. Brenan's niece, Laura, and her husband, Ian, followed.

"Mom is stunned." Dan combed strong fingers through his graying hair. "We pulled off our surprise without a hitch."

Karan grinned and lifted nine-month-old Chrissy onto her lap. Brenan still couldn't believe his sister was a grandmother and that he was a...*great uncle*. But seeing Chrissy, a picture of health, reminded him of the Cambodian orphanage that had clung to his thoughts for some time now. However, he shook off the burden. There wasn't anything he could do to help the missionaries in that part of the world. He'd been called to serve in Brazil...with Elena.

"And here Mom thought she'd spend Christmas Eve alone," Karan said, bouncing the baby on her knee. "Brenan, it's so cool that your plane got in before the bad weather hit."

"Amen to that!"

As the words flowed off his tongue, Mom strode into the room carrying a tray of cookies. Two rosy spots brightened her cheeks, indicating her happiness at this surprise family gathering. Brenan was glad he'd made the effort to come home for the holidays.

"We're going to have another guest." Setting the frosted, decorated treats on the table, Mom straightened. She looked at Brenan. "You'll never guess who's coming."

"Who?"

"Shari Kretlow. Of course, her last name isn't Kretlow anymore. But for the life of me, I can't think of what it is."

"Flannering." Brenan had never forgotten it. While once he rued the day he'd ever heard it, he experienced nothing now as he spoke the surname—nothing other than curiosity. He frowned. "What's Shari doing in Wisconsin? Last I heard, she lived in Tucson."

"Oh, that was years ago, Bren." Karan's voice carried above the baby's squeals. "For the last, oh, I don't know, eight or ten years, Shari's resided in Florida."

"Awful about her husband." Mom shook her head and walked away. "Oh, and Ian," she said to Laura's husband, "would you mind shoveling the walk for our guest?"

"Sure."

Ian stood, and Mom followed him out of the room.

Brenan gazed at Karan. "What about Shari's husband?" It took years before he stopped hating the guy. But he could hardly be about the Lord's work with something like hatred in his heart. Long ago, he made the decision to give all those wrongful, painful feelings over to Christ. "What happened?"

"Don't you read *any* of my emails?"

"Well, I..." Brenan decided he couldn't lie. "I usually skim them, Karan, because I'm so busy."

His sister rolled her hazel eyes in irritation. "Greg died last March. He'd been sick for a long time. Abby told me he'd been out of his mind for the last couple of years and was confined to a nursing home. He used to swear at the nurses and call Shari all sorts of horrible names. But it wasn't really Greg. It was the brain cancer talking."

At another time, one long ago, Brenan might have concluded Greg's decay and demise were poetic justice. Now, however, all he felt was sorrow. What's more, being a medical doctor, he could well-imagine the particulars. "Must have been tough on Shari and all the Kretlows."

Karan nodded as her husband sat down beside her. "In spite of the big scandal they caused when they ran off together, Greg and Shari turned out to be committed Christians. That part has always made Abby nuts."

"Why?"

Karan handed the baby to her daughter, Laura. "Abby believes Shari and Greg gave in to the brainwashing that she grew up with. Now, she says she doesn't even think God exists."

"What a shame." Brenan narrowed his gaze. "So how do you know all this?"

"She does my hair." Karan grinned. "I see Abby about every six weeks and we catch up on all the news."

"Ah." Brenan chuckled, but on the inside a strange, unsettling filled his gut. Shari Kretlow Flannering, once the love of his life, was on her way over...

And she was a widow.

*Two*

SHARI FOUND THE Open Door Inn easily enough and pulled into the back lot as instructed. She noticed the other vehicles parked neatly in a row, although they were now covered with white fluffy snow, and she wondered if Mrs. Sheppard entertained guests after all.

Trudging around to the side of the house on the recently shoveled walk, Shari reached the heavy, ornately carved wooden door. She stomped the snow from her black suede shoes and rang the bell. Miriam Sheppard answered in a matter of moments.

"Merry Christmas!" The older woman enveloped Shari in a hug. "My, my, how good to see you again."

"Likewise. Thank you for allowing me to stay here tonight. I hope I'm not intruding."

"You're not at all. Come in."

Stepping into the large foyer, Shari noticed the gold wallpaper and beautiful dark, polished, tiled floor. Miriam took her coat and Shari watched her hostess hang it in the front closet before she turned her way again.

190

"Let me take a look at you."

Miriam gazed into Shari's face. Their height was evenly matched, and Shari noticed the crinkles around Miriam's eyes and mouth and the deep lines across her forehead. Miriam Sheppard had aged, although she still appeared very familiar as Shari recalled, from her rust-colored hair and brown eyes to her freckled complexion.

"I'd recognize you anywhere, Mrs. Sheppard." Shari chose the polite formality. After all, decades stood between them.

"Please, call me Miriam." She smiled. "And I was thinking much the same thing. You still have that spark of mischief in your eyes."

Shari laughed and the two clasped hands.

"Gracious! Your fingers are like ice. Come on into the living room and sit by the fire."

Shari thought she'd like nothing better. But when she turned to follow Miriam into the other room, her gaze found none other than Brenan Sheppard standing in the doorway. His tall frame cast a long shadow over Shari. Firelight danced off his stylishly cut ebony hair, and he sported an attractive, swarthy mustache and beard. He only vaguely resembled the unmotivated college sophomore she'd dumped for smooth-talking, ambitious Greg Flannering. And, judging by the way Bren's beige cable-knit sweater fit snuggly across his broad shoulders, it appeared he had filled out his once thin physique.

Shari's mouth went dry as she gauged the situation. Was this a setup? A Christmas prank, courtesy of Mom and Miriam?

She grinned inwardly at her deduction and decided to make the best of it. She stuck out her right hand. "Hi, Bren. Good to see you again."

His brown eyes regarded her outstretched hand before meeting her gaze once more. "After twenty-three years, Shari, I don't want a handshake."

Her smile faded. Did he intend to finally tell her off? She'd deserve it if he did.

Brenan grinned. "I want a hug."

Within seconds, he enfolded her into a smothering embrace. She laughed, relieved by the outcome.

"Merry Christmas!"

Brenan released her, although his masculine, spicy-woodsy scent remained on her sweater. Shari stepped back. "Thank you, and Merry Christmas to you too. I didn't know you were back in the States...not that I keep track of your every move or anything." Shari's awkward guffaw hinted at her sudden nervousness, and she quickly explained. "My church supports your missions team, and I read your newsletters every so often."

Brenan arched one dark brow. "What church is that?"

"Golden Shores Community Church in Pensacola, Florida."

"Sure, I'm familiar with it." Brenan's features lit up like holiday lights, and it was obvious he was enthusiastic about his ministry.

Miriam's voice interrupted their conversation. "Shari, come by the fire. I'm sure you're freezing."

Brenan turned sideways and extended a hand, indicating she should enter ahead of him.

Shari complied and walked into the cozy living room. Floral-upholstered furniture was placed in a half-circle in front of a glowing fire that crackled in the fieldstone hearth. One glance to her left said she'd definitely intruded upon a family gathering. However, before she could utter an apology, Brenan's sister Karan jumped up from the settee and strode towards her.

"Shari! Wow, it's great to see you."

Another hug and rare tears gathered in the backs of Shari's eyes. These people should hate her, and perhaps they did at one time. But they seemed to have prevailed over any negative emotions, and now they greeted her with such warmth and sincerity that it touched Shari to her very core.

Karan released her. "You look terrific."

"Thanks." Shari suddenly wished she'd stayed on her diet and lost those pesky pounds rounding her hips. "You look great yourself."

She did, too. Tall and slim, Karan looked like she just stepped out of their high school yearbook. *Totally not fair.* And yet, upon closer inspection, Shari saw the evidence of years past in the smile lines around Karan's brown eyes and at the corners of her red-lipsticked mouth. Moments later, Shari was caught in a flurry of introductions. She met Karan's husband, Dan Strong, their daughter, Laura, and Laura's husband, Ian. Then at last, Shari's gaze fell on a towheaded baby creeping around the plush carpet.

"That's our first grandchild, Chrissy."

"She's adorable." Shari glanced back at Karan and shook her head. "You're about the best looking grandma I've ever seen."

Karan beamed.

"Shari, please sit down," Miriam said, indicating to an armchair close to the fireplace.

She did as the older woman bid her and stretched her arms out closer to the screen, warming her hands. "Maybe it'll stop snowing soon, and I'll be able to drive the rest of the way to Forest Ridge. I'm so sorry to infringe on your Christmas."

"The more the merrier." Karan reclaimed her seat beside her husband.

Brenan sat on the sofa to Shari's left and Miriam on the other side of him.

"I heard the snow's going to keep up through tomorrow," Dan said. He was a nice looking man in spite of his thick midsection.

However, his announcement about the weather plucked an anxious chord in Shari's heart. She had no intention of spending Christmas with the Sheppards, especially since Brenan was in town. It felt too...too weird, awkward.

She stood. "Maybe I'd better try to make Forest Ridge tonight after all."

Brenan pushed to his feet. "That'd be dangerous. You can't drive even that short distance in this snowstorm."

"Bren's right," Karan said. "There's a winter storm warning posted for all of Northern Wisconsin, and the meteorologist on the news at five o'clock advised folks to get off the roads and stay home."

"That was over an hour ago." Shari didn't want to believe her fate. "Perhaps the snow has let up some. I followed a salt truck off the Interstate."

"Shari, I know we just met," Dan said with a grin, "but I'm a bossy guy. Sit down and relax. You're not going anywhere tonight."

Her gaze slid to Brenan who shrugged, and Shari caught an amused glimmer in his cocoa-colored eyes.

She sat and the room fell silent except for occasional squawks from Chrissy.

"Thank you for letting me wait out the snowstorm here." She hoped she hadn't appeared ungrateful for wanting to leave. "Forgive my anxiousness to be on my way. I'm looking forward to being with my family."

"Understandable," Miriam replied.

"Especially after losing your husband, huh?" Karan wore a sympathetic expression. "Abby told me about it after she'd returned from Florida and the funeral. Please accept our condolences."

"Thank you. I did get your sympathy card, but never got around to responding."

Karan waved a dismissive hand in the air. "Not to worry. I didn't expect one."

Brenan sat forward, resting his forearms on his knees. He cleared his throat. "I, too, am really sorry to hear about your loss, Shari. Tonight was the first I learned that Greg passed."

"He would have learned the news sooner if he'd taken the time to read my emails." Karan sent her younger brother a withering, yet sisterly, glare.

Brenan grinned at her before returning his gaze to Shari.

"Thanks," she said once more. "But Greg's in a better place now."

Brenan replied with a thoughtful nod. "Are you...okay?"

"Oh, yeah. I mean, it was such a long, drawn out thing. I actually lost Greg long before he physically died." Shari settled back into the armchair. "But let's change the subject, shall we? This is Christmas Eve, and I already feel terrible about spoiling your holiday."

"Shari, you are *not* spoiling our holiday." Brenan sounded sincere, but authoritatively so. "Now get that idea out of your head."

She saluted, and Brenan cast a quick glance at the ceiling.

Everyone chuckled and, again, Shari was reminded of how much she preferred laughter to tears.

Karan stood. "Shari, would you like to see pictures of your twenty-fifth high school reunion? I was able to go because Carol Baskin couldn't get a date and she didn't want to attend alone."

"Some things never change." Shari smiled at her own quip.

Karan chuckled too but feigned an indignant stance. "Did you hear that, Bren?"

He rubbed his thumb and forefinger up and down his beard-covered chin. "I hate to admit it, but I thought the same thing."

Shari leaned forward and extended her right hand, palm side toward Brenan. He returned the gesture in a modified "high-five" slap.

"You two are despicable," Karan joked as she sashayed from the room. "I'll get the pictures."

❧

"No, she didn't!"

Brenan chuckled as he watched Shari's incredulous expression.

"Vi Taylor married Lyle Koffey? But he was such a dweeb."

"It's the old ugly duckling story," Karan said. "Only it's the male version."

"Hmm..."

Brenan grinned, eyeing the two women as they examined the photos of this past summer's high school reunion. He hadn't been there because of obligations in Brazil, and Shari didn't attend, she said, because she couldn't take the time off of work.

*She's a dental hygienist.*

Brenan let the information digest as he continued to enjoy Shari's exclaiming over every picture. She found something hilarious about each one. Karan was in stitches, and Brenan had to confess to finding Shari quite delightful.

She'd changed a lot over the years, both personality-wise and physically. Gone was that intense, serious, almost angry young lady. Now, Shari's disposition seemed rather larky. She'd put on some weight, but that only seemed to soften her all the more. Her hair was as golden-blonde as he remembered, except instead of long and to her shoulders, she wore it chin length, tucking one side behind her ear. Loopy earrings hung from her lobes and matching bracelets tinkled on her wrists. Shari might turn a guy's head—but not like Elena whose South American beauty could fill a room and draw gasps of awe from anyone within her vicinity. Part of Brenan reveled in the fact that he'd won the prettier woman's heart. However, there was something about Shari he found appealing.

But more appealing than Elena?

He sipped from his mug of hot chocolate and wondered what Shari's life had been like with Flannering. Had she been happy? It appeared so. She'd said she loved him.

"Hey, Shari, did you ever have kids?"

The room grew quiet, and all eyes fixed on Brenan.

He glanced around at the stunned faces. "Did I say something wrong?"

"No, it's just…" Karan groped for words. "Where in the world did that question come from? We're discussing Ted Meinhardt's car dealership."

Brenan stroked his bearded jaw. His cheeks reddened. "Sorry, I wasn't paying attention."

Karan rolled her eyes. "Typical brother. He skims my emails and ignores what I say."

"In answer to your question, Bren…no, I never had kids. Greg and I wanted children, but they never came." Shari shrugged, ignoring her heartache over never giving birth. "*Que sera, sera.*"

"What does that mean?" Laura asked, prying something from the carpet out of Chrissy's chubby fist.

"What will be, will be," Mom piped in as she reentered the room. "Dinner is almost ready." She began to sing the old Doris Day tune. "*Que sera, sera.* Whatever will be, will be…"

Brenan leaned to the side, half-reclining on a throw pillow while Mom soloed down her own Memory Lane. He regarded

Shari, and when she glanced his way, he caught her gaze. "See what you started?"

She laughed.

# Three

AT HIS MOTHER'S request, Brenan brought in the Christmas tree from the covered back porch and set it into its metal stand in a corner of the living room. Karan, sitting on her haunches, arranged the colorful, handmade skirt around it. As tradition dictated in the Sheppard home, the tree was decorated on Christmas Eve and everyone helped. But first, Mom served a dinner of broiled beef tenderloin, twice-baked potatoes sprinkled with paprika, and French-cut green beans.

"Oh, this is delicious."

At Shari's remark, Brenan glanced up from his meal to look across the dining room table at her.

"You're a marvelous cook. Did I always know that or have you improved with age?"

Mom smiled and winked. "I've always been a marvelous cook."

Shari's expression lit up.

Karan cleared her throat. "Shari, did you hear the big news? Brenan's engaged."

Something knotted in Brenan's gut.

Shari's blue eyes widened. "No, I wasn't aware of it." Her gaze flew to Brenan. "Congratulations."

"Thanks, but they're a bit premature." He glanced from his sister to Shari. "I haven't proposed yet."

"But you will and Elena will say yes." Confidence shone on his sister's face. "You said so yourself."

"I'm anxious to meet her," Mom said. "This summer, right, Bren?"

He gave a nod.

"See?" Karan waved a hand in the air. "The proposing part is a mere technicality."

Brenan supposed that was true. His entire missions team expected him to ask Elena to marry him. They were a perfect match, after all. He was a doctor. She was a nurse. They were both unattached and committed Christians—and Elena was crazy about him. What more could Brenan ask for in a woman?

Of course, he was still sort of waiting for that love-struck feeling to hit him. However, he wasn't fifteen anymore and head-over-heels in love with Shari Kretlow, the pastor's kid. The more he recollected, the more he realized that Shari had been one wild young lady back in those days. But Brenan understood why. Pastor Kretlow ran his home like a detention center. The more curfews and groundings he imposed, the worse Shari and her siblings rebelled—and she confided in Brenan about everything. Hindsight told him that he'd simply been a much-needed friend, as well as a frequent voice of reason, although he had loved Shari more than his own being. When he proposed marriage, she'd accepted, solely because she couldn't get out of her parents' home soon enough. Brenan had long ago recognized her motives. On the other hand, he also knew that Pastor Kretlow had mellowed over the years. He'd always loved his congregation, but back then, he behaved more like a tyrant than a father. Even when Shari was in college.

"Brenan, I've got to tell you something."

Her voice drew him from his reverie.

"For years, I've felt burdened for you, and I've been praying that God would bring the perfect woman into your life. You know, it's not good for man to be alone and all that." A smile spread across Shari's face, and Brenan caught her paraphrase of Genesis 2:18. She dabbed the corners of her mouth with her white, linen napkin. "I'm not making this up, either." She shot an earnest look at Karan before glancing back at Brenan. "I'd be happy to show you my prayer journal as proof."

"I believe you and it seems God answered your prayers." He gave a polite smile to hide his mounting discomfort. Wasn't Elena *the perfect woman* for him? When he'd left Brazil, he'd thought so. Then why his sudden skepticism?

"I'll also have you know this blizzard is my fault."

"How's that, Shari?" Mom dipped one rusty-colored brow.

Brenan forked some potato into his mouth as he listened.

"I like Florida, but I miss the seasons, especially snow at Christmastime. So I asked God for a white Christmas." She grinned. "God always answers my prayers, although sometimes He says 'no.' But in this case, He said, 'Let it snow!'"

"Hey, that rhymes." Sitting at the end of the table, beside the highchair, Laura paused with spooning baby food into Chrissy's mouth long enough to chuckle.

"Stop me if I'm being too personal," Brenan began, "but it appears you're a much stronger Christian now than when I last saw you. How'd it all happen?"

"Oh, that's not personal—at least not to me. As you well know, Dad preached the gospel all the time. It wasn't reserved for Sunday mornings. I guess I sort of tuned him out. I got sick of hearing the same thing over and over and over. What's more, I imagined a holy God as a sort of Wizard of Oz-like figure—remember? The guy with the booming voice and big white face?"

Brenan smirked and cut off a piece of his meat.

"Then one night, when Greg was away—" She paused. "He traveled a lot. Anyway, I started watching a Christian broadcast, mostly because I couldn't find another program worth viewing. I began to get curious and wondered what made the evangelist on TV different from my pulpit-thumping father. I watched the entire program, and before long, tears ran down my face. I realized the problem wasn't with my dad at all. It was with me."

When she paused, Brenan looked up and met her remorseful stare.

"I wasn't a Christian when you knew me." Shari glanced around the table. "When you all knew me. Oh, I could talk the talk, but the truth of God's word never penetrated my heart and soul...until that night."

Mom smiled. "Your mother told me years ago. Greg accepted Christ, too, although it was sometime later."

Shari nodded.

"Abby relayed the news to me," Karan said. "But it's sad. She says there is no God."

"I know." Shari nodded her blond head. "The Christmas story, the very reason why God came to earth and was born of a virgin, has been lost on her. Please keep praying for Abby—and for my brothers too."

"Will do," Karan promised.

Brenan felt a bit left out. "Hey, wait a sec. How come I don't know about all this—about Shari and her family?" He glanced first at Karan, then at his mother. "Why didn't anybody tell me?"

"I *did* tell you." Karan's tone held a note of aggravation. "Tonight. Just before Shari arrived."

"You said she and Greg turned out to be committed Christians." He shrugged. "Guess that wasn't much of a surprise." He fixed his gaze on Shari. "I figured the two of you *were* Christians."

"Far from it, I'm afraid. But I wrote you a letter, Bren." Shari sipped her ice water. "Years ago."

"I got it." He stared at his plate and remembered how little comfort it had brought him, how wounded he'd been after reading it. It took a while, but he forgave her—them. "Still, I don't recall you mentioning that turning point in your life."

"Maybe you skimmed her letter like you do my emails," Karan quipped.

A soft chuckle emanated through Shari's pink lips. "I'm positive I told you about it, Bren."

He didn't remember. All that came to mind was her apology for dumping him.

Chagrinned, Brenan cleared his throat. "I'm not a hundred percent sure, but I don't think you wrote about your new faith in Christ."

"Perhaps not. Those blank cards only hold so much information." Her gaze transfixed him from across the dinner table. Then remorse pooled in her blue eyes. "I'm sorry."

"No big deal." He sent her a good-natured wink, but like a hot spot after a raging forest fire, the love he once felt for Shari began smoldering somewhere deep within him. Only now, it was the time to snuff out the last of those feelings for good.

✑

After dinner, Brenan sat on the back hall steps with a string of Christmas lights in his lap. He thought about phoning Elena in Brazil. Hearing her voice would offset the sound of Shari's laughter—at least he hoped so. He glanced at his watch. No, it was nearing midnight. Elena sacked out early and arose at the crack of dawn. Brenan didn't want to disturb her simply because he was having a case of nerves.

Extinguishing the remnants of his affections for Shari wasn't going to be easy. Already Brenan was losing the battle. Sitting across from her at the dinner table fanned some inexplicable eternal flame. After all, Brenan had once promised he'd love her till the end of time—and he'd meant every word.

*This can't be happening…*

He plugged the lights into a nearby electric outlet. Slowly, he began unscrewing each large colored bulb, replacing it with a new one in hopes of finding the culprit responsible for disabling the entire string. For as long as Brenan could remember, fixing Christmas lights had been his job—mostly because he was the only one in the family gifted with enough patience.

From the adjacent kitchen, the sounds of clanging stainless steel cookware accompanied by the scraping of the fine china plates and an occasional clink of glassware reached Brenan's ears. He heard his mother's voice, then Karan's, and finally Shari's soft laugh. Odd, how the latter somehow infiltrated his being and wound itself around his heart.

*Lord, how can I still be in love with Shari after all these years? But…maybe what I'm feeling isn't really love. It's nostalgia.* Brenan's resolve gained strength. That was it—nostalgia. Wasn't it?

Brenan pondered the question. His emotions ran amuck due to the shock of seeing Shari again. And, of course, there was all that reminiscing over high school reunion snapshots.

Chitchat began, and voices were raised over the din of rushing water from the faucet in the kitchen sink. More clanging and scraping. Brenan tried to ignore the ruckus and focus on the Christmas lights. Maybe he would make his excuses and retire for the night while everyone else decorated the tree. He'd spent a good part of the past twenty-four hours traveling. Spending the night in an airplane seat had left him exhausted.

And that's probably why I'm out of sorts. I'm overtired and not thinking straight. He grinned, congratulating himself on finally making the appropriate diagnosis.

"Oh, Shari, I never knew that! Honey, I'm so sorry!"

Mom's sympathetic tone extricated Brenan from his thoughts.

Don't eavesdrop.

"Why did you stay with him?" Karan's louder than average voice rang through kitchen and into the back hall where Brenan sat. "I mean, if Dan cheated on me he'd be dead and I'd be in jail."

Brenan frowned. Had Flannering been unfaithful?

"Oh, honestly, Karan," Mom said, "you say the most outrageous things."

"I'm serious, Mom."

"Listen, I had my own murderous thoughts. Trust me." Shari's voice wafted in to his ears and Brenan couldn't refrain from listening.

Someone shut off the faucet and things grew quiet, including Shari's tone. Brenan strained to hear her.

"But I realized that I made a vow before God, for better or for worse, in sickness and in health, till death shall we part, and I needed to live up to that promise. Because I did, Greg became a believer."

"Abby never said a word."

Brenan rolled his eyes at Karan's remark and unscrewed another bulb. He replaced it. Nothing. On to the next light.

"I kept Greg's infidelity from my family, although they're aware of it now. But back then, I was afraid they wouldn't support me in my decision to stay with Greg. And I didn't want to, but when he returned home after his fling and said he'd been diagnosed with a brain tumor, it seemed almost inhumane to turn him away—especially since I carried the health insurance."

"Oh, mercy!" Mom exclaimed. "You've really been through the wringer, haven't you?"

"Tried by fire is how I term it."

Shari actually laughed, surprising Brenan.

"I like to think of myself as pure gold now," she added.

Brenan couldn't help a grin, and he caught Shari's reference to Job's trials and tribulations in the Old Testament.

"Do you think you'll ever remarry?" Karan asked.

Brenan hated the way his ears perked up.

"I don't know. It takes a long time to train a husband."

All three ladies chuckled.

Brenan shook his head.

"Besides," Shari added, "the world is full of such weirdoes—even within the Christian community. That may sound harsh, but God warned his children about wolves in sheep's clothing. I'm here to tell you they really exist. Take the last date I had. Now, mind you, I haven't dated in more than two decades, but..."

Shari's voice became nothing more than a whisper. Seconds later, shrieks of disbelief followed by raucous laughter bounced off the plaster walls and ping-ponged into the back hall. Brenan didn't think he could stand much more. His emotions were in a jumble. His heart went out to Shari for enduring her husband's unfaithfulness without the support of her family while, at the same time, he admired her strength of character. He suddenly wanted to know more about her. In a word, he was...interested.

All at once, Brenan felt like a guy who'd stepped into quicksand, and he was sinking fast. Up to his knees, to his chest— pretty soon he'd be a goner.

*Lord, help!*

The string of lights in his lap suddenly went on. *Thank You, Jesus!* Yanking the cord out of the socket, he stood and traipsed through the breakfast nook. He paused when he reached the main part of the kitchen.

The women sobered when they saw him. Surprised expressions lit their faces.

"I think it's sin to have so much fun doing the dishes," he teased, careful not to meet Shari's gaze. He held the lights up to his mother. "All fixed."

"Wonderful. Thank you, Bren."

After a nod, he proceeded into the living room, hoping to busy himself. No doubt, Dan and Ian would help rid his mind of those unexpected, superfluous thoughts about Shari.

# *Four*

SHARI WANTED TO disappear. "Do you think he heard us?"

"Naw." Karan sent her a dismissive wave. "Bren doesn't listen to small talk. I mean, look how he tuned us out when we were rummaging through those high school pictures. We were all in the same room and he couldn't even keep up with the conversation."

Shari hoped Karan was right, although she'd glimpsed an odd expression on Bren's face before he strode out of the kitchen. Had it been pity? Or was it satisfaction? Except...didn't Bren see that he'd have never gone on to medical school if he'd married her? It all worked out for the best.

"Elena, being a nurse, must talk his language, because..." Karan shook her head. "If women are from Venus and men are from Mars, then Bren's got his very own planet."

"Oh, nonsense." Miriam continued loading the dishwasher. "Bren merely has an incredible mind. Smart as a whip. That's why he's such a marvelous doctor."

Shari smiled, recalling he'd always been a good student. She probably wouldn't have graduated high school if Brenan hadn't helped her.

Pushing up her sleeves, she rinsed plates and salad bowls and handed them to Miriam. Next, Shari washed the remaining pots and pans. Karan dried them and put them away.

At long last, the ladies ambled into the living room. The first thing Shari noticed was Chrissy fussing in Laura's arms. Shari spotted the exasperation pinching the younger woman's features, and her heart went out to her.

"Can I hold the baby?"

"If you want to." Laura glanced at her daughter then back at Shari. "She's awfully crabby. Happens every night before bedtime."

Shari gathered Chrissy into her arms, and Laura handed her a crocheted, pink blanket and a pacifier. The child squawked, but Shari rocked her from side to side and began singing soft strains of "Away in the Manager." Chrissy quieted and stared curiously into Shari's face. Seating herself on the couch near the fire, Shari wrapped the blanket snugly around the little one. Minutes passed while she rocked and sang to the baby. Miriam, Karan, and Laura unpacked boxes of decorations. Since she'd barged in on their Christmas Eve, tending to the baby was the least Shari could do. Besides, she never passed up an opportunity to hold an infant.

Shari went through her repertoire of lulling Christmas songs. "Silent Night," "It Came Upon A Midnight Clear," "O Come O Come Emmanuel," and her favorite, "O Holy Night."

Laura strode across the room and peered down into her now-sleeping child's face. "She so sweet and innocent. Who'd believe she's such a terror by day?"

Grinning, Shari decided Laura favored her mother in appearance, right down to her trim figure and hazel eyes.

"You got her to sleep." She stared at Shari. "How'd you do that?"

Pleased by the compliment, Shari shrugged a reply. "I do have a way with kids. The nursery workers at church adore me."

"I can see why. Will you come and live with me and do this every night?"

Noting the teasing note in Laura's voice, Shari laughed softly.

Laura moved to take Chrissy, but Shari touched her forearm. "Can I hold her a while longer?"

"Sure. Give a holler when your arms are about to give way. Chrissy's a pretty solid kid."

"I'll holler…but not too loudly."

Laura's eyes widened and peered at Chrissy. "Right."

She returned to assist her mother and grandmother trimming the tree. It already sparkled with multicolored lights and glittering ornaments.

Shari sighed. A glowing fireplace, a sleeping baby in her arms—life didn't get much better than this.

*ℰℐᴖ*

Brenan leaned on the heavy oak doorframe, his arms folded across his chest, and watched Shari rock his great niece to sleep. Since he stood just outside her line of vision, he could regard her unnoticed, and Brenan couldn't help feeling jealous of Chrissy, snuggled in close, the lilt of Shari's soprano voice soothing her into a deep sleep. In fact, Brenan's eyelids grew heavy, and he seriously contemplated making his excuses and retiring to his bedroom. But another tradition in the Sheppard family was reading the Christmas story from the Gospel of St. Luke. Dan had been awarded that privilege, much to Brenan's relief. Fatigue peaked, and he could barely see straight let alone read from the family Bible.

Brenan blinked, spotting Mom's orange tabby, named Sunkissed, hop up on the couch. The animal nestled himself next to

Shari, and Brenan realized she had that way about her, attracting both people and pets. Greg had been daft to risk his marriage for what Shari termed "a fling." And Shari...she was one remarkable woman to take him back, and all to God's glory. Brenan couldn't get over it. He kept thinking about it, much to his irritation.

As if his legs had minds of their own, he found himself strolling toward the sofa. He scooped up Sunkissed, setting him on the carpeted floor. The cat meowed in protest, but Brenan ignored the feline and seated himself beside Shari.

"Hey, that wasn't nice, Uncle Bren. Sunkissed was dozing."

He glanced at his niece who held a gold garland in her hands. "Would it have been better if I sat on her?"

Laura gave him a glare but quickly turned back to her task of tree trimming.

"My apologies for any offense, Laura." He smirked. "But I've always believed that furniture is for people and obscure corners, preferably outside, are for cats."

Laura hurled a glance upward, and Mom snorted her amusement.

Karan muttered, "Typical Bren."

Beside him, Shari grinned. "You never did like cats, did you?"

Turning to his right, he met her blue-eyed stare. "Nope. Never did."

Her smile widened at his admission before she glanced down at the sleeping baby in her arms.

Bren stretched his arm out along the top of the sofa and reached across Shari's lap with the other to caress Chrissy's soft cheek. "Babies look so angelic when they're sleeping."

"Yes, they do."

"And this girl is a very healthy little angel." He grinned and straightened. "But each time I look at her, I feel this inexplicable burden for an orphanage in Cambodia." Brenan couldn't be sure why he was telling Shari all this, although it seemed the right thing to do. "I learned about the place from a fellow missionary. Children, some as young as newborn babies, are left at the doorstep. Many are sick and need medical attention, but the ailments are usually curable."

Shari's mouth dropped slightly open. "They're left at the doorstep of the orphanage? Abandoned?"

Brenan nodded. "Usually it's a family member—a grandmother or distant relative—who has been left the responsibility of caring for the child for one reason or another. Due to the extreme poverty in that country, many can't afford to pay for healthcare. Even if they could, qualified physicians are hard to find."

Shari's gaze turned misty. "That breaks my heart."

"Mine too."

"You and Elena must go and help care for them."

Brenan smiled at Shari's determination. "We'll see." The truth was, Elena didn't want to leave Brazil and her people. Many of them were in as much need as the poorest of Cambodians.

"What's to see, Bren? Those children need you. God didn't put that burden on your heart for nothing."

He couldn't quell the grin tugging at his mouth and finally gave in. Shari always had been something of an advocate for the underprivileged. In high school, she'd befriended the kids whom others picked on.

Like himself. Brenan was the guy who wasn't good at sports, a little awkward and clumsy—until he'd grown into his feet.

At that moment, Dan and Ian sauntered into the living room and sat down. Dan set the family's large, black Bible on the coffee table, an indication that he was ready to read the Christmas story whenever Mom announced it was time.

Brenan crossed his leg, right ankle to left knee, as light chitchat ensued. Meanwhile, Mom, Karan, and Laura finished decorating the tree. A good while later, Laura took Chrissy upstairs to the portable crib.

"Remind me, Dan. Do you and Karan have other children?" Shari smoothed out her black dress over her knees.

"Two sons. Both in the Army." Dan's expression was a mix of pride and remorse.

"I cried for a week after they went off to boot camp," Karan said from across the room. "That's where they are now. But they should be here with us."

"Now, Karan..." Dan sent her an understanding glance. "They'll be back."

"How old are they?" Shari inquired.

"Eighteen and twenty." Dan shifted his weight in the armchair.

Moments of silence passed before Shari turned to Brenan. "Hey, Bren, tell me about Brazil. As I said before, I've read your quarterly newsletters, but tell me the inside scoop."

He grinned. "What inside scoop?"

"What's your apartment or house like? What are the people like?" She arched a conspiratorial brow. "How'd you meet Elena?"

Everyone hooted.

"That's what she *really* wants to know, Bren." Daniel laughed again.

Shari's face turned the color of her red sweater. "Okay, so I'm nosy. That's old news."

Brenan's smile grew. "Elena is a nurse at the hospital where I work."

"And?" Shari prompted.

"And...what?"

"How did you start...dating? Was Elena walking down the hallway, taking care of somebody, and you asked her out?"

"Actually, she was angry with an uncooperative patient. Out of frustration, Elena hurled an empty bedpan across the room. I happened to be entering at that precise moment to witness all the yelling. Fortunately, I ducked before getting clocked upside the head."

Shari burst out laughing, causing Brenan to chuckle.

Standing near the tree, Karan whirled around and strode toward him. "How come you never told Mom and me that story?"

He lifted his shoulders and laughed again, mostly because Shari was still giggling beside him.

"Guess you just have to ask the right questions." Ian gave a toss of his blond head with a wry grin.

"So she got your attention, eh?" Shari's smile lingered on her pink mouth.

"I suppose you could say I got her attention. Elena felt so ashamed for losing her temper that she apologized about five times. Finally, she asked if she could make me dinner in recompense for her deplorable behavior. I agreed. Things progressed from there."

"Smart woman." Shari raised one eyebrow. "She knows the way to a man's heart is through his stomach."

While others found the remark amusing, Brenan didn't. He studied the seam on his trousers. The truth was that Elena hadn't found her way to his heart. He thought she had, but it seemed someone else still occupied that special place.

He looked at Shari. Her blue eyes glimmered as she met his stare.

"Did she do the whole soft music and candlelight thing?"

Feeling oddly mesmerized, Brenan found it hard to even muster a smile. "Candlelight...yeah."

"Dude, you should have sensed trouble right there," Dan quipped.

Positioned directly behind him, Karan smacked the top of her husband's head. "Marriage is blissful. Remember?"

"Oh, yeah. Glad you reminded me."

More chuckles filled the room.

"All right, everyone, I think it's time for the Christmas story." Mom reentered the living room, and her announcement capped further discussion. "Just as soon as Laura returns from putting the baby to bed, we'll begin."

Dan slid the Bible onto his lap and flipped it open.

Shari leaned closer to Brenan. "I'm sorry if I embarrassed you. Sometimes I get carried away."

"No harm done." He smiled and moved his hand from the back of the couch to her shoulder. He gave it a squeeze, an effort to assure her. But seconds later, he brought his arm back to his side. He shouldn't touch her. He shouldn't even sit next to her. Even the same room was too close a proximity, and yet he couldn't get himself to budge.

"I'm really happy for you, Bren."

Her words crimped his heart, and he realized that somewhere in the deepest recesses of his being, he didn't want Shari to be "happy" about his impending engagement to Elena.

He wanted Shari to love him.

# *Five*

"SO IT WAS, that while they were there, the days were completed for her to be delivered. And she brought forth her firstborn Son, and wrapped Him in swaddling cloths, and laid Him in a manger, because there was no room for them in the inn."

As Shari listened to Dan read from the Gospel of Luke, she tamped down anguished thoughts of those poor children left on the orphanage's doorstep in Cambodia. She tried to pay attention to the Christmas story but found herself asking Jesus to protect those helpless kids on the other side of the world. Wouldn't Shari enjoy telling *them* the Christmas story and about how much Jesus loved them! She would probably want to adopt every single child she met.

An idea struck. Maybe she could adopt one of those orphans. Would it be allowed since she'd be considered a single mother?

Shari decided to ask Brenan about it later. Perhaps he could put her in touch with that "missionary friend" he'd mentioned.

She forced herself to relax and tuned into the Bible reading.

"And behold, an angel of the Lord stood before them, and the glory of the Lord shone around them, and they were greatly afraid. Then the angel said to them, 'Do not be afraid, for behold, I bring you good tidings of great joy which will be to all people. For there is born to you this day in the city of David a Savior, who is Christ the Lord...'"

Shari marveled as she always did whenever the reality hit her. The Word—being God—became flesh in order to save mankind from sin and eternal death. What a wonderful Savior to leave His heavenly home and be born by the lowliest of births.

Shari's eyes grew misty as Dan finished reading. She peeked at Brenan, only to find his brown eyes regarding her with interest. Giving him a tentative smile, she wondered what he was staring at. Lipstick on her teeth? Mascara dripping down her cheek?

She looked back at the others. No one else regarded her oddly. Glancing back at Bren, she gave him a smile. He was still very much that quiet, introspective man she'd known so long ago. It gave her an odd sense of gratification that, in spite of the years distancing them, she could draw him out of his shell.

When the reading was finished, Brenan touched her shoulder. Again, Shari turned to face him.

"Are you still a coffee drinker?"

She nodded.

"If I make a pot of decaf, will you drink a cup or two?"

"Sure." She smiled.

Brenan stood and left the living room. Maybe now would be a perfect time to ask him about the orphans and his missionary friend.

Following him into the kitchen, Shari paused at the doorway while Brenan scooped coffee grounds into the filter. She took that moment to collect her thoughts until Brenan saw her and grinned.

"Can I get you something?"

"Um, no. I wanted to ask you about that orphanage."

"Oh? What about it?" Brenan walked to the sink and filled the carafe with purified water.

"I wondered if I could get more information about it, specifically about adopting a child. I've wanted kids for so long, and things never worked out before. But I'd be a single mother. Do you think this orphanage would consider me qualified and...first things first, does the facility even allow adoptions?"

"I think they do." Brenan poured the water into the automatic coffee maker and then flipped the power switch. "Tom and his wife already adopted two kids."

Shari willed herself not to feel prematurely optimistic. How many times in the past years had her hopes been dashed when it came to having a child of her own?

Too many to count.

Brenan's smile widened as strode toward her. Without warning, he leaned forward and pressed his lips to hers. His soft beard brushed lightly against her face as the moment lingered. To her surprise, the kiss warmed her insides more than a cup of hot coffee.

"Merry Christmas," he whispered, straightening.

"Merry Christmas," she murmured back, stunned by what had just occurred.

As if in explanation, Brenan flicked his gaze above her head. "Mistletoe."

She looked up and gave a nervous little laugh. "Oh..."

His soft chuckles filled the space around them.

"Okay, you got me. I never saw it coming, and I never noticed the mistletoe up there." She glanced up again, and in that time, Brenan's arms encircled her waist. Wide-eyed, she stared back at him. His dark brown eyes peered down at her, warm and rich with a hint of longing.

Shari sobered and put her hands on his chest, pushing him back. "No, Bren...we shouldn't."

He released her. "You're right."

A flash of hurt entered his eyes, and she caught the sleeve of his sweater before he turned away.

"Bren?" She frowned. What could he possibly be thinking by kissing her?

He swallowed before replying. "I guess it's seeing you again, Shari."

Heartsick at the idea that she might have ruined more than his Christmas Eve, Shari wondered about leaving. "I'm sorry..."

Brenan rubbed the backs of fingers over her cheek. "And that's the problem—I'm not."

"But—"

Before she could ask him about his fiancée waiting for him back in Brazil, Karan burst into the room.

Brenan took a step back, and Shari felt as if they were mischievous teenagers again, kissing on the sneak like they did at age fifteen.

"Mom made chocolate mint pie. It'll go great with the coffee." Karan smiled at Shari. "Want to help me slice and serve?"

"Absolutely."

Guilty as original sin, Shari cast a glance at Brenan, but he was already making his way back to the rest of his family. She wasn't certain of all that had just happened between them, but one thing she knew for sure. Shari wasn't about to stand in the way of Brenan's happiness a second time.

What in the world had possessed him to kiss Shari?

Brenan lowered himself onto the sofa while conversation droned on around him. He didn't hear a word anyone said as he berated himself for being so impulsive. It wasn't his nature, and yet he couldn't seem to help it. Shari standing in his mother's kitchen, under the mistletoe, her pink lips puckered in thought—she'd looked too good to resist.

Brenan glanced at the entryway as Karan strode into the living room, carrying a large tray. He stood to assist, but Ian beat him to it.

"Shari went up to her room," Karan announced while handing out coffee and cake. "She has a headache, and I can understand why. The poor dear drove all the way from Indiana today and she's beat."

Brenan wasn't surprised at the news, except he'd bet it was his kiss and not a headache that caused Shari to retire for the night. He'd be lucky if she ever spoke to him again.

"Ian, would you be a sweetheart and bring in Shari's luggage?" Karan placed a set of keys in her son-in-law's palm. "She needs the blue suitcase that's in the trunk."

"Will do." The younger man grinned and reached for his wife. "I never pass up a chance to play in the snow."

Laura giggled and took his hand. Together, they walked off.

"Bring the luggage in first," Dan hollered after them. He shook his head. "Kids."

Brenan felt a tad envious of his niece and Ian, just like he'd felt envious of Karan and Dan over the years. It seemed everyone in his family had someone—someone to have and to hold...and to play with in the snow. Everyone except for him.

"Do you think Elena would like the snow?"

Mom's question yanked Brenan from his self-pity. "Not sure."

"Hmm..." She furrowed her brows. "Something bothering you, Bren?"

"Yeah." He set his untouched slice of cake onto the tray. "But perhaps I'll have a new perspective on things tomorrow. I'm exhausted." He stood. "I think I'll turn in for the night."

"We're not far behind you." Karan sipped her cup of decaf. "I feel pretty whipped myself."

Brenan forced a smile then kissed his mother's cheek before wishing Dan and his sister a good night.

As he climbed the stairs, he rued his foolish heart. Talk about perverse human nature. Beautiful Elena awaited him in Brazil. But no, she wouldn't do. Instead, his heart longed for a woman who didn't return his affection—Shari, the woman who would never love him back.

# *Six*

SHARI LAY IN the darkened bedroom, listening to the wind howl outside. She kept reliving Brenan's kiss. Odd, how his kisses hadn't affected her when they were teens. But tonight's surprise smooch left her senses reeling.

Even so, Shari was determined not to give in to her longings. What's more, the realization that her premonition was correct all these years caused a swell of guilt in her chest. Brenan hadn't married because she'd hurt him so badly.

*Oh, God, please heal his heart. Isn't he in love with Elena? If he is, then why did Bren say he wasn't sorry after he kissed me?*

A gust of wind whistled around The Open Door Inn, and Shari snuggled deeper into the blanket and quilt on her bed. Once more, Brenan came to mind, and it pained her to think her very presence tonight had wounded him all over again. As for herself, Brenan's kiss had awaked something deep inside of her. She couldn't recall the last time she'd been in a man's arms for a sweet, romantic interlude—and her last date with *Mr. Octopus* didn't count. What a sick twist of fate that now, when she felt attracted to Brenan, he wasn't available.

But, maybe he could be…

No! No! No!

Shari reined in her foolish thoughts. If she came between Brenan and Elena, the Sheppards would regard her as that same selfish, rebellious woman she'd been twenty-three years ago. Karan would tell Abby, and Shari's Christian testimony would be at stake. How would she prove to her siblings that Jesus was as real as Greg's illness had been if Christ couldn't be seen in her life?

On that thought, Shari closed her eyes and allowed the exhaustion from driving all day to overtake her.

⁓

The next morning, Brenan awoke early. He showered, dressed, and then phoned Elena. He hoped that hearing her voice would alleviate his doubts about them as a couple. But instead of Elena, her roommate, Dori, answered the phone. At twenty years old, Dori was the youngest on the team. Spunky and likeable, she taught school for all the missionaries' kids.

"Elena's not around. She left for the weekend with a group of others. They're celebrating Christmas by skydiving over Rio de Janeiro and hiking into the Amazon."

Brenan sat forward and frowned. "Elena's doing…*what?*"

"Skydiving. Tomorrow they trek through the jungle." Dori giggled. "You know them, Dr. Sheppard. They're crazy."

Yes, he knew. He was keenly aware of the five daredevils working at the hospital, although he hadn't thought Elena was one of them.

"You couldn't pay me enough to jump out of an airplane—unless it was about to crash or something."

Brenan grinned at Dori's remark. "Thank you for the information. Please tell Elena—and the rest of the team—that I called to wish them a Merry Christmas."

"Will do. But, um, is that everything you want me to relay to Elena?" Dori's voice took on a teasing, singsong tone. "No three little words, perhaps?"

Brenan took the hint. However, the only *three little words* that he longed to say were, "Yes, that's all."

He ended the call and sat back in the armchair in the corner of the bedroom. He thought about how well Elena and Dori got along and struggled again with the age difference between Elena and him. And it wasn't her daring that troubled him. Skydiving actually sounded fun, and he'd already hiked through parts of the Amazon with a tour guide. It was Elena's apparent footloose attitude that caused Brenan to rethink his marriage proposal. He didn't want to spend the remainder of his life trying to tame an energetic and overly zealous wife. What if he didn't succeed?

Lowering his head, he prayed. Elena was beautiful in more ways than just her physical appearance. She loved Christ, and Brenan sensed she wouldn't refuse his proposal of marriage. He was attracted to her, and he'd probably learn to love her. Shouldn't that be enough?

Perhaps, although it wasn't.

And then, of course, there was Shari...

Brenan confessed his attraction to her also, although his feelings for Shari ran so much deeper than those for Elena.

*Lord, now what do I do?*

❦

"You can't leave without breakfast!"

Shari blinked at her hostess' exclamation. Standing near the back hall, her suitcase in tow, Shari was all set to trudge out to her car, clean off the snow, and drive to her parents' house. The storm had passed. She'd said goodbye to Karan, Dan, Laura, and Ian, thankful that Brenan wasn't around. But when she entered the kitchen to thank Miriam for allowing her to stay overnight, the older woman halted Shari in her tracks.

"I'm baking cranberry muffins. Karan made a delicious egg, cheese, and sausage bake. Please stay." Miriam wore a beseeching expression.

Shari's resolve crumbled. She didn't want to appear ungrateful, after all. "Well, it does smell awfully good in here."

Miriam beamed. "Let me get you a cup of coffee."

Minutes later, cup and saucer in hand, Shari was escorted into the dining room where Laura fed baby Chrissy.

"I didn't think you'd get away that easily," Karan teased. "Mom has this thing about feeding people."

Shari chuckled lightly. "So I've discovered."

"And she won't let anyone help her cook, either, although she did grant me the privilege of creating my Italian egg bake."

"It sounds scrumptious."

"You'll love it, Shari," Dan piped in.

Karan relayed the recipe and Shari listened with a smile while she sipped her coffee. The egg dish sounded easy enough to put together, and the beauty of it was it could be prepared the night before.

At last, Miriam brought out warm cranberry muffins. A short time later, she carried in the rectangular, glass baking dish containing Karan's culinary masterpiece. Brenan followed his mother to the table, and a nervous little flutter tickled Shari's insides.

"Merry Christmas, everyone."

Shari replied with a tight grin, as her gaze wandered over him—black jeans, a forest-green pullover that accentuated his muscular chest…did Brenan work out?

Shari shook herself. Mercy! What was wrong with her?

She sank her gaze into her coffee cup.

"Morning, Shari."

"Morning, Bren." She felt his scrutiny. Her face began to flame.

"Merry Christmas, bro."

Shari glanced up in time to see Brenan grin at Karan. Shari almost sighed audibly that he'd removed the weight of his stare. But then, to her discomfort, Brenan took the chair beside her. As he sat, his shower-fresh, spicy-woodsy scent wafted to her nostrils. She found it most appealing, and suddenly, Shari felt doomed.

Well, she'd eat to appease Miriam, but she'd make it quick. Afterwards, she was out of here.

"Let's all hold hands and ask the Lord's blessing," Miriam said from the head of the table.

*Nooooooooooo!* Shari's mind screamed. But, out of a sense of propriety, she smiled at Brenan and offered her hand.

He took it in a firm but gentle grip.

"Ian, will you pray for us?"

"Sure."

*Make it fast!* Shari bowed her head, closed her eyes, and tried to concentrate.

"Thank You, Lord, for our meal and for family and friends. Thank You for coming to earth two-thousand years ago and conforming to the image of a man in order to save our souls. Thank You for…"

Shari stymied a groan as the younger man's prayer droned on for what seemed like hours while her hand was held captive in Bren's.

Finally, Ian wrapped it up. "We ask Your blessing on this food and on this Christmas Day as we remember Your birth. Amen."

"Amens" were murmured around the table. Brenan gave Shari's hand a small squeeze before releasing it. His gesture sent a zinging up her arm that went straight to her heart.

Moments later, plates were passed as Miriam served everyone a healthy portion of the egg bake. Shari began to eat, forcing herself not to gobble so she could hightail it out of The Open Door Inn and Brenan's disturbing presence.

"So, Shari..."

She glanced at the object of her tumultuous thoughts. "Yes?"

"What made you decide to become a dental hygienist?"

She swallowed the food before it stuck in her throat. "Um, well...I was working at a dentist's office as a receptionist and realized that with some additional training, I could just about triple my wages. So I went back to school, got my license and...and that's how it happened."

"Do you enjoy it?"

"Sure." Shari sipped her coffee, hoping it would wash down her emotions. "Pays the bills."

"Bet you've got a lot of them, what with Greg being so ill and all."

Shari looked across the table at Karan who'd made the remark. "Actually, I don't have many medical bills at all. I'm blessed with premium health insurance through my job, and Greg was awarded disability coverage through the State of Florida. Of course, I don't own a house. That was the first to go after Greg got sick."

"That's right. Abby said you live in a two-bedroom apartment." Karan wiped her mouth with a red paper napkin. "She told me it's in a nice complex with a pool and a clubhouse."

Shari nodded. "I'm very comfortable, and somehow, I squeeze my family into my place when they visit." A laugh slipped out as she recalled last year's Christmas holiday when her two brothers slept in sleeping rolls on the living room floor. Two nieces and Luke's wife had crowded into Shari's queen-size bed. Shari and Abby slept on the floor nearby so their aging parents could occupy the guest room. The next morning, none of the adults except Shari's mom and dad could move. However, their sore muscles served as great excuses for jumping into the hot tub.

"You've been through so much, Shari. But your trials made you a strong woman." Miriam smiled while spreading butter on half of her muffin.

"Oh, I don't know how strong I am." She thought of how weak-kneed and nervous she was at the moment, sitting beside Brenan. She tried not to look for his reaction, but out of the corner of her eye, she saw him give her a smile.

Finally, Shari couldn't stand it anymore. She scooted her chair back. "I need to get going. Thank you for breakfast...thanks for everything."

"You're welcome, dear, but must you leave so soon?" Miriam's disappointment shone on her age-lined face.

"My family's expecting me."

Her hostess gave a nod. "So good to see you again."

"Likewise."

Brenan turned in his seat. "Before you go, Shari, why don't you follow me upstairs to Mom's desk-top computer? Something's wrong with my laptop, and I'm sure she won't mind if I use it to print off information on the Cambodia ministry I told you about last night."

*The adoption possibility.* How could she possibly forget about those poor children on the other side of the world?

"Bren, of course you can use my computer." Miriam sipped her coffee. "But mind yourself with that printer. It's been giving me fits lately. Jams up every so often."

"Thanks for the warning." Brenan slid back his chair and stood. Placing his palm beneath Shari's elbow, he helped her to her feet and guided her unnecessarily toward the stairway. "Tom built a pretty elaborate website. I think you'll find it extremely informative."

"I'm sure I will."

Together, they climbed the steps and entered Miriam's large bedroom. In one corner was a nook in which a computer desk fit almost perfectly. Brenan booted up the machine then pulled over a second chair. Shari sat down, forgetting all about her anxious, fluttery emotions. A swell of hope replaced them. God obviously had a reason for allowing her to stop here last night in the middle of a blizzard. Perhaps that reason had something to do with adopting a Cambodian orphan. Maybe the Lord would finally bless her with that one thing she'd never been able to attain, no matter how hard she prayed—

A child.

# *Seven*

ENGROSSED, SHARI EXPLORED the web site. She learned *Hollia's House*, the Cambodian orphanage, was named after a little girl who died of leukemia. Hollia's parents were part of the American missions team that began the work a little more than five years before. After viewing the smiling faces of some of the youngsters and reading their stories of how they came to live at *Hollia's House*, Shari wanted to adopt them all.

"Bren, this site states that many of the children at the orphanage are in need of medical care—like Hollia, who succumbed to her cancer."

"I know what it says." He leaned back and stretched his arm out along the top of Shari's chair. "Tom's been after me to join his ministry for the past three months."

Shari sat back too. "Why the hesitation?"

"For one, I want to be sure it's God's will for me. There are a lot of worthwhile causes in the world. I can't take on all of them."

"True." Shari glanced down at her dark brown corduroy slacks and began to fidget with a piece of lint.

"Number two reason is Elena doesn't want to leave Brazil."

Shari's gaze adhered to Brenan's. "Ahhh. Yes, I see where that might pose a problem."

"And that's not the only problem..."

Brenan stared at the computer monitor. His profile was so familiar to her, yet so strange, especially with the addition of that well-groomed, inky-black beard. She imagined it would feel more soft than scratchy beneath her fingertips.

She gave herself a mental shake. What was she thinking?

Refocusing on their conversation, Shari's common sense told her to leave the subject of Elena alone, but she couldn't seem to do it.

"What's the additional problem, Bren—if I'm not being too nosy?"

He regarded her then leaned closer, as if about to divulge a very personal secret. "For some time now, Elena has been talking marriage. Each time she broached the subject, I'd get what I can only describe as a check in my heart. I've discussed the matter with my pastor who told me I've merely been single too long. I'll get over it." Brenan took a deep breath. "I've been trying, but that check doesn't go away."

"Did you mention this to Elena?"

Brenan shook his head.

"That might be a good place to start."

"You're probably right. But..."

"But? What's the problem?"

Brenan expelled a weary-sounded breath. "Talking won't fix one of my biggest concerns. It's the difference in our ages."

Shari felt an odd twinge of jealousy. "How young is she?"

"Just turned thirty."

"Thirty isn't *that* young, Bren." Shari quelled her envy. "Look at it this way...she's still got many childbearing years ahead of her."

*She can give him a family and I can't.* Shari shook off her wayward thoughts. Why did she think of herself? She had no part in this equation.

"I'm not so concerned about the childbearing part of Elena's age," Brenan said, recapturing Shari's attention. "What makes me wary is her slightly irresponsible behavior. Elena acts more like she's twenty. I don't want to become some sort of father-figure to my wife. If I marry, I want a partnership. Camaraderie. I think a husband and wife should be on the same emotional and spiritual level."

"Well, yeah, that's the way it's *supposed* to work." Shari curbed her guffaw and tore her gaze from Brenan's earnest brown eyes. "But I'm afraid I'm no expert in that area. For half my marriage, I was blissfully ignorant of reality, believing Greg loved me the way I loved him. But one day I got this phone call—"

She halted.

"Go on," he urged. "Tell me."

Brenan's tone was filled with such compassion that Shari didn't think twice about continuing. "One day, I received a phone call from a woman named Annette Ellison. She was *the other woman*. One of them, anyway. She discovered Greg had a wife and, as a way of getting even, she decided to contact me and divulge the whole ugly truth about her affair with my husband."

Brenan winced.

"And here I thought he was away on business, working hard, missing me while he slept alone in his hotel room. The truth was he'd been staying with her. They even rented an apartment together. Greg lied to me and to Annette, saying he was working when he'd come home to me." Shari smacked her palm against her forehead. "Stupid me. I never suspected a thing."

"Aw, Shari, I'm so sorry."

She shrugged. "It's all over now." She ran her thumbnail over her slacks, a nervous gesture. "But maybe I got my comeuppance, huh?"

After throwing out the challenge, she chanced a peek at Brenan and studied his expression, gauging his reaction. But all she saw in his handsome face was empathy.

"I wouldn't wish that kind of heartache on my worst enemy." He slipped his arm around her shoulders and gave her a hug. "And I never thought of you as my enemy, Shari. Greg, maybe. You, never."

His soft voice and gentle words, his nearness, and embrace, seemed to penetrate her very soul. Lifting her hand, she touched his cheek, and her fingers found their way to his silky beard. Their gazes locked, and Shari thought she could drown in his brown eyes.

But suddenly reality hit. *What am I doing?*

She shot up off her chair. "I have to go."

"Shari, wait..."

She didn't, but instead hurried across the room and out the bedroom door. Running down the steps, she prayed Brenan wouldn't follow. She found her coat in the closet, grabbed her purse, and called a goodbye as she hustled passed the dining room.

"Thanks for everything!"

"Whoa, Shari, wait up a sec."

She ignored Karan's request and grabbed the handle of her suitcase, still in the back hall.

"Good seeing you, Karan."

"But...I want to ask you about New Year's Eve." She jogged through the kitchen to catch up. "Good grief, where's the fire?"

Shari's face flamed. "Don't ask."

With that, she bolted out the door and to her car.

⨏

From his mother's second-story bedroom window, Brenan folded his arms and watched Shari unbury her car. Snowflakes swirled in the winter air, and he prayed she'd make it safely to her folks' place before the next storm hit. As disappointed as he was, watching her go, a newfound sense of hope plumed inside of him. He recognized the longing in her eyes—it mirrored his own. She fought the same battle he did—but why? Had she determined that all men were like Greg and not trustworthy?

Brenan considered various scenarios and concluded he could spend all day guessing. He'd have to pray. Only God could change Shari's heart—and his too.

*Lord, I think I still love her. Is that possible? Most of all, is it Your will?*

"Bren, what did you do to Shari?"

Hearing the reprimand in his sister's voice, he pivoted towards the door and faced her. "What do you mean?"

"You know." She huffed and set her hands on her hips. "You scared her. What did you say?"

"Karan, I think..." Brenan stroked his beard and pursed his lips momentarily. "I think Shari and I sort of scared each other."

She narrowed her gaze and stepped toward him. "I don't get it."

He shrugged. "I don't either, but I'd like to pursue the matter." He headed for the door, skirting his sister.

"Pursue the matter? As in...you and Shari?"

Brenan glanced over his should and grinned. "Me and Shari...kind of has a nice ring to it, don't you think?"

At Karan's wide-eyed, gaping expression, he chuckled all the way downstairs. Even as a kid, Brenan had enjoyed riling his older sister. He especially liked to get in the last word.

Ah, yes, some things never changed.

"Merry Christmas!"

Shari threw her arms around her mom and dad. Next came her brothers, followed by Abby and her husband. Finally, she embraced her sister-in-law Rebecca and nieces and nephews, Elizabeth, Crystal, Madeline, Andrew and Alex.

Shari expelled a sigh of relief. "I'm so glad to finally be here."

"Ditto. Your mother worried you'd get stuck in another snowstorm," Dad said with a wide grin. At age sixty-nine, his dark blond hair now silvery gray, Walt Kretlow still stood as tall and willowy as ever. The sound of his voice hadn't changed much either. It still rang with authority, but his features had softened. "Glad to see that wasn't the case."

"Me, too, although those last few miles were difficult. Roads are pretty slick."

Mom shooed everyone out of the delicious-smelling kitchen. Dough was rising in the automatic bread maker, and a beef roast cooked in the oven.

"When can we open presents?" Four-year-old Madeline ran into the kitchen. She'd inherited Luke's blond hair and blue eyes.

"Soon," Mom promised. She smiled at Shari. "The kids are so impatient."

"That's to be expected. It's Christmas." Shari hugged her slender mother again. "It's good to be home."

"It's good to have you home."

Arm in arm, they made their way through the small house and into the living room. Shari drank in the sight of her family, noticing two were missing. Her brother Mark's kids.

"Where's Ashlee and Jack?"

"Deidre's got 'em," Mark groused.

Shari's heart did a nosedive, not so much because the kids weren't here, but at her brother's tone. Mark and Deidre were in the process of a nasty divorce and, judging from the last few times she'd talked to him, Mark grew more angry and bitter as it progressed.

Lowering herself into one of the overstuffed armchairs with its red and green throw, Shari considered her younger brother as he sat on the couch. Remote in hand, he surfed through the TV channels. He stopped when the kids squealed over a program they enjoyed watching.

The phone rang and Mom strode from the room to answer it.

"So how was your drive up, other than hitting snow north of Milwaukee?

Shari turned to her lovely sister-in-law Rebecca and smiled. "Other than the storm, I made good time."

"How was your stay at the Sheppards' bed-and-breakfast?" Abby asked. "Kinda boring, I imagine, with just Miriam there."

"Actually, Karan and Dan were there along with Laura and Ian and their sweet little girl Chrissy, and, um..." Shari turned and scratched the back of her head. "Brenan was there too."

"Get out of town!" Abby leaned forward, and under the lamplight, her hair shone with a purplish hue. Being a stylist, she was always doing something trendy to her short hair. "Brenan was there? Was it, like, World War III or something?"

"Not at all. We got along great." *Maybe a little too great.*

"You mean he didn't even make mention of how you dumped him?"

"Abby, that was a lifetime ago. Bren and I were fine. Everything was fine." Shari hoped her no-big-deal tone belied the tumult raging inside her.

"Fine?" Mark pinned her with an incredulous stare. Sitting forward, his forearms on his thighs, his hands dangled over his knees. "Shari, if I was Brenan, I'd never want to see your face again and, if I did, there'd be trouble."

Shari blinked, shocked by his vehemence.

"I'm merely being honest."

The minister in Dad suddenly emerged. "Brenan is a Christian, Mark, and Christians forgive those who trespass against them."

"Yeah, whatever." He sat back on the sofa and crossed his leg. Wearing faded jeans and a gray sweatshirt, Shari thought her brother appeared somewhat disheveled. His light brown hair had outgrown its last cut, and his chin was bristly, as though he'd forgotten to shave this morning.

Mild trepidation gripped her. Was he letting himself go? Had he lost hope? Faith?

"So, Shari, how is Bren these days? My, my, it's been a good number of years since I've seen him last."

At her father's inquiry, she pushed out a smile. "Oh, he's doing just fine."

"There's that word again," Abby remarked. Sitting beside her husband, Bill, she arched a brow. "Somehow I don't think things were as *fine* last night as you say."

Shari waved off the notion. "Oh, I'm tired, Abby, that's all."

Mom appeared at the doorway. She was all smiles. "Guess who just phoned? Brenan Sheppard. It was like old times, hearing his voice just like when he used to call for Shari."

She wanted to groan but kept a rein on her emotions.

Mom looked right at her with that all-knowing parental stare. "Bren wanted to make sure you arrived safely. He said he was worried about you—isn't that sweet?"

Shari grinned, willing her cheeks not to redden with embarrassment.

"He also said to tell you that he printed the information you wanted off the Internet and he'll give it to you tomorrow at church." Mom clasped her hands with glee and peered across the room at her husband. "Isn't that marvelous? Bren and Miriam are coming to our Sunday service tomorrow."

"Wonderful." Dad sported a pleased expression.

"Afterwards, I invited them here for lunch."

"Not really, right?" Shari tried not to visibly grimace.

"Oh..." Mom frowned, obviously sensing Shari's discomfort. "Shouldn't I have done that? I'm sorry. I thought by the way Bren was talking that you were friends."

"We are." Shari moaned. "Oh, don't mind me. I'm exhausted and not thinking straight. Of course it's all right that Bren and Miriam come over tomorrow. Miriam was the perfect hostess last night and this is your home."

"Was Bren a good host?" Abby smirked.

Shari tossed a glare at her sister.

"Can we open presents now?" Andrew asked, leaning against his dad. The boy was Abby and Bill's eldest son, and Shari decided he was growing more handsome each year.

"Walt, what do you think?" Bill asked. "Can the kids rip and tear?"

Shari grinned as her father chuckled and nodded. "Have at it, kids." His gaze spanned the room and he smiled. "Now that Shari's here safe 'n' sound, it's really Christmas!"

# Eight

SHARI SQUINTED AS morning sunshine streamed into the room she shared with her niece, Elizabeth. Christmas Day had come and gone pleasurably, and today was the Lord's day. She figured it was her bad luck that another snowstorm wasn't blowing through Door County right now, keeping Brenan and his mother at home. Nope. They'd be in attendance at the service today.

Tossing off the bedcovers, she stood and strode across the cold wooden floor and down the hall to the bathroom. She showered and dressed, changing clothes three times before deciding on a black skirt and a colorful, coordinating button-down sweater. As she took care in applying her cosmetics, she tried to convince herself she wasn't out to impress Bren.

But if that was true, why didn't she tell her family about Elena, the woman waiting for him back in Brazil?

Shari stared at her reflection, hating the turmoil in her heart. She felt a stab of jealousy each time she thought of *the other woman*. Or was she *the other woman*? Regardless, and as sinful as it might be,

Shari secretly wished things wouldn't work out with Elena and Bren. But then she despised her wayward emotions all the more.

*Oh, God...* Shari closed her eyes. After she and Greg ran off, she'd prayed for a wife for Bren. God had answered that prayer with Elena. So why couldn't Shari be happy for him—them?

After a quick breakfast, Shari rode to church with her parents. Luke and Rebecca followed in their family-sized sport utility vehicle, loaded with the three kids. Once they arrived, Shari helped her mother prepare two large urns of coffee for the brief fellowship that followed the service in the basement of the quaint country church. Shari had forgotten how small the structure was in size. It seemed miniscule compared to the church she attended in Florida.

Mom wiped her hands on a nearby towel. "That ought to do it. Shall we head upstairs?"

Shari nodded, but dread filled her being at the thought of coming face-to-face with Brenan.

"What's wrong, dear?"

Shari gave herself a mental kick before sending her mother a smile. "Nothing's wrong. Nothing at all."

"Sharon Rose, I know you too well." Mom's blonde brows knitted together in a frown. "Something's bothering you. What is it?"

For about five seconds, she considered confiding in her, but then realized Mom would fret the rest of the day. No, best to keep things to herself.

Shari covered by laughing it off. "I'm being silly, that's what it is. It's been eons since I've seen a lot of the people who'll be here today. I'm a bit nervous."

Immediate relief washed over Mom's features. "Oh, don't worry about anything. Folks wonder how you're doing all the time. Dad and I stay busy trying to keep 'em up to date."

Still smiling, Shari followed her mother into the tiny vestibule. Several individuals, whom Shari didn't recognize, were hanging up their winter wraps. While Mom stopped to chat, Shari wandered into the sanctuary. Already, her brother Mark sat in a pew next to Luke, Rebecca, and their kids. Abby would show up soon with her husband, Bill, and their brood. While the minister's offspring rarely darkened this church's door, they had decided to gather together today out of respect for the Christmas holiday and their father.

Shari strode across the sanctuary. She chatted with several of her parents' friends, and then a gentleman whom Shari had never met started playing the organ so loudly, it drowned out their discussion. Wishing folks a good day, she made her way to the pew in which her brother sat. Noticing that Abby had arrived and was busily seating her children, Shari looked for a place to squeeze in and still leave room for Mom.

It was at that moment that Shari glimpsed Brenan and Miriam strolling up the aisle. She hated the way her heart leapt at the sight of him, although he was a head-turner in that charcoal suit coat and red necktie. Despite her inner turmoil, she managed to smile a greeting.

Brenan nodded. "G'morning, Shari."

"Morning."

He grinned when she continued to stare at him until Shari realized how stupid she must seem and tore her gaze from his bearded face.

"Bren!" Abby's exclamation rivaled the organ. "My long-lost big brother!"

He chuckled as she gave him a quick hug. She pulled him forward and introduced Bill. Mark and Luke stood and clasped hands with Brenan. Miriam was soon sucked into the throng.

The organ quieted, but the welcome committee did not. Shari's father appeared at the pulpit and cleared his throat before grinning out over his congregation. "As you can see—and hear—my grown children and little grandchildren are in attendance today."

Laughter filled the sanctuary, and Shari could tell her father was thrilled that everyone showed up. Tossing a smile at him, she turned to take her seat but realized there wasn't a space left for her beside Abby. Of course, if her sister would kindly move her purse and scoot in closer to Bill...

"No room here, sis. You'll have to sit back there." Abby indicated the pew behind her by thumbing over her shoulder.

Shari's gaze bounced to Miriam and Bren, then back to her younger sister's smug expression. "No problem, Abb." She wasn't about to let on that sitting beside Bren was the last thing she wanted to do. She refused to appear rude either.

Stepping alongside the end of the pew in which Brenan sat, she pushed out a smile. "Mind if I sit here?"

"Course not." Bren slid over, forcing his mother to do the same.

She took her place. But the instant her arm brushed his, the last of her defenses crumbled.

Abby twisted around and handed back Shari's Bible, still in its leather carrying case. Brenan politely reached for it and gave it to Shari.

"Thanks."

He smiled.

Her heart skipped a beat.

"It's also nice to have Miriam Sheppard here, along with her son, Brenan," Dad said. "For those unware or who've forgotten, Brenan is a doctor, and he's serving the Lord in Brazil as a medical missionary." Walt waved him to the platform. "Why don't you c'mon up and say a few words, Bren?"

242

He inclined his head in reply.

Shari rose and stepped aside to let him out and claimed the spot next to Miriam so she wouldn't need to get up again.

"The Lord is really doing a great work in Brazil," Brenan began. "I'm privileged to serve with the team over there. They primarily help the impoverished folks who live in *favelas*, or slums. There's a real need in that part of the country." He paused. "But lately, I've sensed God's call to a different corner of the world, and I'd appreciate your prayers on this matter."

Brenan flicked a glance in her direction, and something of a thrill spiraled up Shari's spine.

"There is an orphanage in Cambodia that I'm burdened for. I'm acquainted with the man who runs it, and he's been pleading with me to come and help with his ministry. The children at the orphanage are in dire need of medical care. Here are some specifics."

He pulled something from the inner pocket of his suit coat. Was it the information he'd printed off the Internet for her?

"The orphanage cares for some one hundred and fifty children, but that number is growing by the day. An estimated one hundred and forty *thousand* children in Cambodia are orphans, having lost their parents to suicide, AIDS, and any number of illnesses and infections plaguing the malnourished and extremely poor in that region. Some children are disabled, like the twelve-year-old girl I was told about. She'd been helping her mother harvest rice and stepped on a mine that was left over from the Khmer Rouge days. Consequently, she lost a leg. Other children live with hunger and severe malnutrition. They don't have homes, families, or education, nor are they offered healthcare. They appear on the doorstep of the orphanage dirty and often suffering with any number of tropical diseases."

Tears welled in Shari's eyes. Her heart constricted as she listened to the plight of the orphans.

"A good number of kids come with behavioral problems due to the years they lived with abuse or neglect—or both. In short, these children need Jesus Christ. They need to hear about salvation through Him. They need hope. Ministry goes well beyond helping to heal diseases and repairing wounds. There is a spiritual aspect to it that I don't take lightly. But the question is, does God want me in Cambodia?" Brenan's gaze scanned the congregation. "That's why I ask you to pray—and please remember *Hollia's House* in your petitions also." He inclined his dark head ever so slightly in thanks.

Shari sniffed and wiped the moisture from her tear-stained cheeks. Miriam handed her a Kleenex, extracting one from her purse for herself too.

Brenan strode from the pulpit to the pew and sat beside Shari. He glanced over and sent her a polite little grin.

She dabbed her eyes. "You did a wonderful job up there—really conveyed the need of the hour."

He answered with a diminutive but grateful nod.

"I'm glad you and Elena are thinking about helping that orphanage."

Brenan leaned over and whispered, "Elena won't be coming."

"Oh?" Curious, Shari tipped her head. But before she could inquire further, her father's voice filled the sanctuary.

"Thank you, Dr. Sheppard. Now, let's stand and sing our first hymn. 'Angels We Have Heard On High.'"

Shari stood, as did Brenan and Miriam along with the rest of the congregation. From her vantage point, Shari caught sight of her brother, Mark. His gaze lingered on her face before moving to Bren. Finally, he glanced at his hymnal and sang with everyone else, but

Shari found the nonverbal exchange rather odd. What was Mark thinking?

It was then that Shari recalled his struggle with forgiveness as a result of the ugly divorce proceedings he faced. Perhaps he wondered how Bren could forgive her after she'd run off with Greg a lifetime ago. As she sang, Shari closed her eyes and prayed her brother and sister-in-law would reconcile. While the words of the familiar Christmas carol tumbled from her lips, she lifted up the orphans in Cambodia to her Heavenly Father. Her heart crimped with a longing to help them all.

"...in excelsis De–e–o."

The song ended, and Shari lowered herself into the pew that suddenly seemed to have shrunk. Glancing to her right, she saw that Karan and Dan, along with another family, now occupied the space on the other side of Miriam, forcing her to move over, which in turn caused Shari to sit even closer to Brenan.

She relished his nearness. But far be it from her to ruin his life with Elena. She glanced upward. Nothing short of divine intervention could fix this mess.

# Nine

AFTER THE SERVICE, Shari and Abby ducked out of church as the fellowship downstairs began. Brenan had been snagged by folks who wanted to learn more about the orphanage, and Shari had to admit she wanted additional details. However, she'd promised her sister they'd help their mom by preparing lunch before the Sheppards arrived. Now that Karan and Dan were coming to lunch as well, she and Abby needed to set two extra places at the dining room table.

"You know, I think Bren still has feelings for you."

Shari glanced at Abby who placed silverware around the table. Following her with a stack of plates, Shari digested the remark and wondered how to reply. She had feelings for Brenan too, but what would their families think of her disrupting Brenan's well-laid plans a second time?

*Except Bren did say he had a "check in his heart" about marrying Elena...*

"Shari?"

She glanced at Abby.

"You know what? If you and Bren got back together, I might even believe there's a God."

Shari was momentarily dumbfounded. "Why do you say that?"

Abby shrugged and set down the last of the silverware. "I always thought Brenan Sheppard was the perfect Christian—if there could be such a thing. I idolized him when I was a kid. He was like the big brother I adored when my real big brothers picked on me and teased me."

Shari smiled. "I never knew you thought of Bren that way."

"I did. And when you ran off with Greg, I hated you for a long time."

Shari winced.

"But I got over it," Abby continued. "I grew up and figured out that Christians were more like our dad than Bren, and I learned that most romances ended like Romeo and Juliet's and not like the ones in fairy tales. Then I met Bill. He's a great guy, trustworthy, honest, makes a decent living. I figured he was the best I'd find out there—and, don't get me wrong, I love him. But it's like I keep waiting for the day to come when he doesn't want to be married anymore, or, like Deidre, he decides he's got more important things to do in life than be a spouse and take care of a family."

Words escaped Shari. She longed to alleviate Abby's fears, but she didn't know Bill that well—and look what happened with Greg.

Abby walked around the table and came to stand right in front of her.

"I can tell that Bren's faith is real. Dad's is too, even though he's made a lot of mistakes. But it's different with Bren. His faith shows on his face and it's heard in his voice. I mean, when he was talking today about those kids in Cambodia, I felt like hopping a plane and adopting the whole orphanage."

Shari smiled. "Yeah, me too."

Abby gave a nod. "And seeing you and Bren together today gave me some hope that maybe there is such a thing as everlasting love." Abby's gaze darkened with intensity. "He obviously still loves you. I saw it in his eyes when he looked at you. And you've been distracted ever since coming home yesterday saying everything was 'fine.'" Abby snorted. "Fine, yeah, right. You're still in love with Bren too."

"Maybe so." Shari all but whispered the reply, fearing the fallout such an admission might bring.

But before she and Abby could discuss the matter further, the back door banged and children's voices echoed through the otherwise quiet little house. The hungry troops had arrived.

In the kitchen, Shari helped Mom ready the meal, relieved that Brenan gave her some space. He hung out with Mark and Luke in the living room and, judging from the chuckles emanating from that area of the house, they were enjoying themselves.

When at last they sat down for the noon dinner, Mark seated himself between her and Brenan. Once more, Shari was glad for the buffer. The tightness in her neck ebbed as she relaxed, and soon she actually enjoyed the company.

After they'd finished eating, there was talk of snowmobiling. Brenan said he'd brought along a change of clothes, suspecting the rowdy Kretlow boys would engage him in some sort of outdoor activity. Dan opted to watch the football game on TV with Dad and Bill while Shari decided to make herself useful in the kitchen again. But on her way in, she encountered her brother and niece.

"Daddy, you promised." Large tears rolled down Elizabeth's cheeks.

"Oh, stop it. You go ice skating all the time."

Shari clucked her tongue. "Luke, how can you not be persuaded by that sweet face pleading with you?"

He smirked. "Those are crocodile tears. She turns 'em on and off like the bathroom faucet."

"Dad-dy!" Elizabeth cried all the harder.

"Oh, you poor thing." Shari gathered her niece in her arms and hugged her close. "You're so mean, Luke," she teased. "You broke your daughter's heart."

"Yeah, Daddy."

"You'll get over it." He narrowed his gaze at her. "Shari, for your information, all these kids know you're a big pushover."

"Of course I am. I'm the aunty." She stroked Elizabeth's blondish-brown hair. "What are aunties for? Now, what do you want, sweetheart?"

Shaking his blond head, Luke walked away, and Elizabeth sniffed. "I want to go ice skating this afternoon. My friends'll be at the rink and Daddy said he'd take me and Crystal."

"I'll take you."

"Goody!" The nine-year-old's tears vanished so quickly it amazed even Shari. Pushing out of her embrace, the girl ran through the house, rounding up her sister and two cousins.

Luke appeared, dangling the keys to his truck. "Four kids won't fit in your car."

Even though there were five kids in the house, little Madeline was too young to take part in this outing, but Luke was right. Four children couldn't safely ride in her compact car.

"Use our vehicle."

Shari accepted the proffered keys, wondering if maybe her niece had succeeded in manipulating her this time.

Climbing the steps, Shari exchanged her black skirt and heels for black jeans and insulated hiking boots. When she returned downstairs, Bren was waiting for her.

"Want some company?"

Shari halted. "You don't want to snowmobile?"

He shrugged. "I thought we could talk while the kids skated."

Shari's heart hammered inside her chest, and staring into Brenan's gingerbread-colored eyes didn't calm it in the least. She felt so torn, wanting to spend time with him, yet wondering if the idea was wise. Could a relationship between them be God's will? Everything was happening so fast.

Gazing into her palm at Luke's keys, she figured it was foolish to forestall the inevitable. They needed to talk. Their attraction to each other was obvious—so much so that even Abby had noticed. Perhaps discussing things would help set them both in the right direction.

"Sure, come along. I'd love the company and..." She tossed Brenan the keys, smiling. "You can drive."

&#x222B;&#x2044;&#x2323;

Brenan hadn't forgotten the way to the ice rink. He'd skated there as a kid, although now, according to Luke, a brand new warming house had been erected, complete with a snack bar that served steaming coffee and hot chocolate.

Driving through Forest Ridge, the town in which he'd grown up, Brenan noted the changes, some subtle, some not so subtle—like the movie theatre. That building went up in the last decade or so, but the restaurant he and all his buddies used to hang out at in their high school days still occupied the corner, although its name had changed.

"Do you have fond memories of this town, Shari?" he asked over the din of the chattering kids in the back of the truck.

"Yes, for the most part." Her smile lit up this cloudy afternoon.

So how did he go about putting into words what he wanted say? There was a chance that Shari would reject him a second time, and he did his best to prepare himself for that worst-case scenario.

They arrived at the ice rink, and the kids sprang from the vehicle and ran for the warming house. In a flash, they returned with their skates on and headed back outside.

Brenan purchased two cups of coffee and walked over to where Shari had found seating on the bleachers facing a large plate glass window that allowed parents or guardians to supervise and spectators to observe the skaters. He handed the steaming brew to her and sat beside her. He wondered again how to he might begin to voice his innermost thoughts.

"Bren?"

"Hmm?" He glanced her way.

"You said this morning in church that Elena wouldn't be going to Cambodia with you—that is, if you even go. Can you tell me why?"

He almost breathed a sigh of relief. Leave it to Shari to get the ball rolling. "Elena phoned me last night from the hotel where she and some others on our team were staying. We wished each other a Merry Christmas and then I told her in the nicest way I knew how that I wasn't returning to Brazil."

"What?" Shari turned so fast that her knee knocked his.

He grinned at the incredulity widening her eyes. "I'm not going back. Even if God closes the door on the ministry in Cambodia, It's not meant for me to return to Brazil."

"But...what about your belongings? Don't you need to pack your stuff?"

"I don't own all that much, and what little I do possess, the team will pack and ship to me."

"Are you…well, are you afraid of seeing Elena again? Maybe meeting with her will stir up your feelings and—"

"No, that's not the case. I'm not afraid to see Elena." Brenan thought his *once bitten twice shy* theory might be correct after all. Shari didn't want to get hurt again, and who could blame her. "I respect Elena and she's a beautiful person, a fine sister in Christ. Last night I complimented her on becoming an outstanding nurse. It's been a privilege to work with her."

"But?"

"But…" Brenan leaned closer to her. "Shari, I've sensed all along something wasn't right between Elena and me. Now I know what it is. I don't love her."

"No?"

"No." His gaze locked with hers. "I'm still in love with you."

Before Shari could reply, male shouts filled the warming house. Brenan glanced over her head. A man stood at the entrance wearing a wild-eyed expression and began shouting. "Someone call the paramedics. My daughter's been hurt and I think she stopped breathing!"

# *Ten*

"HERE SHE COMES. She's regaining consciousness."

Shari knelt on one side of the child and Brenan on the other. The little girl had taken a tumble on the ice, and an older boy behind her accidentally stepped on her fingers with his skates. Afterwards, the wounded child stood but passed out, scaring her parents half to death.

"Did she hit her head?" Brenan queried.

"I'm her mother and no, she didn't." The woman hovered over them wearing a troubled look. "Angie was crying after she fell, but no sound came out of her mouth. Then her lips turned blue and she collapsed."

"Could be that the pain from her injury caused your daughter to black out." Brenan gave the mother a reassuring grin before inspecting the girl's pupils. "Angie, can you hear me? I'm Dr. Sheppard."

She blinked and stared up at him with large brown eyes.

"Can you hear me?"

At last, she nodded.

While Brenan continued his examination, Shari packed snow around the child's wounded hand. She guessed Angie's fingers were broken, although her thick mitten had provided a good amount of protection. The injury could have been worse.

A small crowd gathered, and someone said the ambulance was on its way. Shari watched as Brenan interacted with the youngster. He reassured little Angie, telling her everything would be okay. He asked what her favorite color was and if she had brothers and sisters. Answering his questions successfully distracted her. At one point, she even smiled. When the paramedics arrived, Shari and Brenan moved out of the way.

"Thanks a lot, Dr. Sheppard." The girl's father stuck out his right hand. A red ski hat with yellow trim covered his head, but his face was ruddy from the cold December wind. His expression, however, reflected his relief and gratitude.

Brenan shook the man's hand. "Glad I could help, although I really didn't do much."

Shari stood by, watching the exchange. Brenan had done more than he realized. His soothing presence and air of confidence evoked calm in everyone surrounding the girl, and yet there wasn't an arrogant bone in Bren's body.

Paramedics took the child off the rink and to the hospital. Normalcy returned, and the skating continued. Shari's nieces and nephews wanted to skate a while longer, so she and Brenan headed for the bleachers again. Several people approached them, asking about what had happened, and Bren gave brief explanations so as to protect the girl's medical confidentiality as best he could, given the witnesses. Shari was impressed by his professionalism.

Waiting for him to return to his seat beside her, Shari recalled his admission. She could hardly claim surprise. She'd suspected that

Bren still loved her since Christmas Eve. But her mind was in a whirl. She couldn't think straight.

Before they got another chance to talk, the kids finished their skating. Brenan drove back to Shari's folks' home. They arrived and learned that Karan and Dan had left and they'd taken Miriam with them.

"Looks like you're stuck here for dinner," Dad told Brenan with an amused snort.

Brenan replied with a good-natured shrug. "If dinner is as tasty as lunch, I'm a happy man."

Mom's cheeks turned pink from the compliment, but a determined glint entered her gaze. "Count on that tasty dinner, Bren."

"Shari can drive you home later." Dad said.

"Well…" Brenan hesitated and flicked a glance in her direction. "Only if she doesn't mind."

"Of course I don't mind, silly." She rapped him on the upper arm before sauntering off to the kitchen. But her easy reply belied the knot in the pit of her stomach. So much was still unsettled between them.

Later, after dinner, as she carried a tray of frosted, decorated Christmas cookies into the living room, Shari spotted Brenan outside on the patio, talking with Mark who smoked a cigarette. She noticed her brother appeared very attentive to whatever Bren was saying.

"Shari, did you just hear me?"

She shook herself. "What?"

Luke chuckled. "I said Bren's still a great guy."

Her heart did a flip, but she managed to set down the dessert tray without knocking something over. "Yeah, he is."

Abby's words from earlier in the day came back to Shari. Seeing you and Bren together today gave me some hope that maybe there is such a thing as everlasting love.

Her family would approve of the match, not that she needed their approval at forty-three years old. Still, she coveted it, and they'd welcome Bren back into the family with open arms. She turned back to where he and Mark conversed outside. Their breath sent white puffs into the frosty air. Could it be that God was answering her prayers with regard to family members who needed a good shot of faith right now? Could it be that He used Bren for that mission?

❧

Shari stuck her key in the ignition of her car and the engine roared to life, perhaps a bit louder than she preferred, but her vehicle started. What more could she ask for? She drove a ways and didn't even reach the Interstate before the words poured from the depth of her soul.

"Bren, I'm unsure of what's happening."

"What do you mean?"

"About us. You said you still love me, but—"

"Shari, I realize I put you in a bad position and I apologize. But I can't help how I feel, and I thought you needed to know."

She mulled it over as she drove to the Sheppards' bed-and-breakfast. Neither spoke the rest of the way.

At last, they reached The Open Door Inn. Shari parked, and before she could say another thing, Brenan reached over and set his hand on top of hers.

"Thanks for the lift home. Maybe we'll talk sometime this week." He opened the car door and hopped out so fast, it jarred Shari's senses. She didn't want to part on such an uncertain note.

"Brenan, wait." She killed the motor and climbed from behind the wheel. She watched as he backtracked until he stood only a foot away, his hands stuffed into the pockets of his navy-blue, down jacket.

"You didn't put me in any sort of bad position. I'm just...confused, I guess. You're a wonderful guy and we have so much in common. We're both burdened for the same ministry." She wracked her brain, searching for the right words to express all the tumult inside of her. "Bren, I want you to understand something..."

"You're scared." Brenan stepped closer and cupped her face. His palms felt warm against her cold cheeks. "Greg betrayed you, but, Shari, I would never hurt you. I'd die before I would ever break your heart. You don't ever have to worry about my loyalty. I think I've always been devoted to you."

"I believe you." Tears clouded her vision. "But what about your mom and sister? Will they think I'm the same selfish woman who wounded you once and now ruined your chances of happiness with Elena?"

"What?" Brenan brought his chin back. His brows furrowed. "My mother and Karan love you, Shari. They always have. I talked to my family last night after getting off the phone with Elena. Mom said she suspected all along that I still loved you."

"Really?" His words were like a healing salve on her wounded spirit. "Oh, Bren, I think I love you too. Wait. I take that back." She collected her wits as he patiently waited. "Bren, I'm positive I love you too. Perhaps I always have, but I didn't recognize it back then."

Beneath the glow of the multi-colored outdoor Christmas lights, Shari watched the smile spread across his face. Stepping forward, he folded her into his arms and kissed her. Shari felt more cherished and secure than she could ever remember.

"I swear I'll never hurt you again, Bren."

"I know you won't." He rested his temple against the side of her head. "And I'm not in any hurry, either. I've waited this long for you, Shari, I can wait a little longer if you want to make sure."

She smiled, deciding Brenan Sheppard was a rare gem, a golden nugget along a stony pathway.

Moisture began settling on her lashes, nose and cheeks. She blinked and looked up. Fat snowflakes swirled in the frozen night air and landed on her face.

"What is it with this stuff?" Shari stepped back and gazed into Brenan's bearded face. She noticed his dark hair glistened with dusty flakes. "It's snowing again!"

"Yeah, looks like you're stranded here. Too bad, huh?"

Shari laughed. The light snowfall was hardly a major winter storm.

Brenan gave a nod, indicating his mother's home behind them. "Plenty of room at this inn."

There was nowhere else she'd rather be than curled up beside Brenan while a log crackled in the fireplace. "You're right." She threaded her arm around his. "I'd better not drive in this *blizzard*."

"Smart move."

Arm in arm, they walked to the house, and Shari thought of the tune she'd heard on the radio a few nights ago. She hummed several bars and then, together, she and Brenan sang…

"Let it snow, let it snow, let it snow!"

# Karan's Italian Egg Bake

2 dozen fresh eggs

1 small finely chopped onion (optional)

1 small finely chopped green pepper (optional)

¼ cup butter or margarine

1 cup milk

½ teaspoon salt

¼ teaspoon pepper

½ cup cooked and crumbled Bob Evans sausage or Italian sausage (or cooked and crumbled bacon)

½ cup shredded Italian cheese (or cheddar or mozzarella)

¼ cup finely chopped fresh mushrooms (optional)

¼ cup finely chopped fresh spinach (optional)

### Directions

Melt butter and pour into 13 X 9 pan, making sure to well coat bottom and sides of pan.

Next scramble the eggs and milk then add desired remaining ingredients. Mix well. Pour into pan. Cover and let the egg mixture sit overnight in the refrigerator.

In the morning, bake egg mixture uncovered in 350 degree oven and bake it for 30-40 minutes. Allow it to stand for 5 minutes before cutting and serving. Eat and Enjoy!

Serves approximately 12-15.

# About The Author

Andrea Boeshaar has been married for nearly forty years. She and her husband have three wonderful sons, one beautiful daughter-in-law, and five precious grandchildren. Andrea's publishing career began in 1994. Since then, 30 of her books have gone to press. Additionally, Andrea cofounded ACFW (American Christian Fiction Writers) and served on its Advisory Board. In 2007, Andrea earned her certification in Christian life coaching. She speaks at women's retreats and leads writers' workshops. For more information, log onto Andrea's website at: www.andreaboeshaar.com.

Follow her on Twitter: @AndreaBoeshaar

"Friend" her on Facebook: Andrea Boeshaar Author.

Thank you for your Prism Book Group purchase! Visit our website to enjoy free reads, great deals, and entertaining, wholesome fiction!

http://www.prismbookgroup.com